the Cheetah girls

Hey, Ho, Hollywood!

Deborah Gregory

JUMP AT THE SUN

HYPERION PAPERBACKS FOR CHILDREN

NEW YORK

Fashion credits: Photography by Charlie Pizzarello. Models: Imani Parks, Mia Lee, Brandi Stewart, Arike Rice, and Jeni Rice-Genzuk. On Imani (Dorinda): leopard dress with red trim by Daang Goodman for Tripp, NYC. On Mia (Galleria): pink and black dress by XOXO, satin Mary Janes by Steve Madden. On Brandi (Chanel): brown velvet snake-print dress by Daang Goodman for Tripp, NYC. On Arike (Aquanette): black dress by Mica. On Jeni (Anginette): gray velvet leopard dress by Betsey Johnson. All gloves by LaCrasia. All hosiery by Look From London. Hair by Jeffrey Woodley. Makeup by Lanier Long. Fashion styling by Sharon Chatmon Miller.

Printed in the United States of America
First Edition
5 7 9 10 8 6 4
This book is set in 12-point Palatino.
ISBN: 0-7868-1387-3
Library of Congress Catalog Card Number: 99-61156

For my brother, Edgar Torres,
The cheetah-licious "E.T."
Ah, yeah, that's he
Rocking on a thing called the M.I.C.
The M.I.C., well, that's a microphone
And when he rocks it to the beat,
It's rocked to the doggy bone!

The Cheetah Girls Credo

To earn my spots and rightful place in the world, I solemnly swear to honor and uphold the Cheetah Girls oath:

- Cheetah Girls don't litter, they glitter. I will help my family, friends, and other Cheetah Girls whenever they need my love, support, or a *really* big hug.

- All Cheetah Girls are created equal, but we are not alike. We come in different sizes, shapes, and colors, and hail from different cultures. I will not judge others by the color of their spots, but by their character.

- A true Cheetah Girl doesn't spend more time doing her hair than her homework. Hair extensions may be career extensions, but talent and skills will pay my bills.

- True Cheetah Girls *can* achieve without a weave—or a wiggle, jiggle, or a giggle. I promise to rely (mostly) on my brains, heart, and courage to reach my cheetah-licious potential!

- A brave Cheetah Girl isn't afraid to admit when she's scared. I promise to get on my knees and summon the growl power of the Cheetah Girls who came before me—including my mom, grandmoms, and the Supremes—and ask them to help me be strong.

- All Cheetah Girls make mistakes. I promise to admit when I'm wrong and will work to make it right. I'll also say I'm sorry, even when I don't want to.

- Grown-ups are not always right, but they are bigger, older, and louder. I will treat my teachers, parents, and people of authority with respect—and expect them to do the same!

- True Cheetah Girls don't run with wolves or hang with hyenas. True Cheetahs pick much better friends. I will not try to get other people's approval by acting like a copycat.
- To become the Cheetah Girl that only *I* can be, I promise not to follow anyone else's dreams but my own. No matter how much I quiver, shake, shiver, and quake!
- Cheetah Girls were born for adventure. I promise to learn a language other than my own and travel around the world to meet my fellow Cheetah Girls.

the Cheetah girls

Chapter 1

The plastic slipcover on the couch makes a real loud *crunch* sound when Galleria sits down. Me and Angie are used to the funny noise so we pay it no mind, but Galleria looks kinda embarrassed like she farted an "Alien egg," or something strange like that. Me and Angie just look at each other and smile because we're probably thinking the same thing. That's how it is when you're twins—you can read each other's mind, finish each other's sentences, *and* know when each other is "lying, crying, or testifying," even when you're not in the same room.

My sister Angie and I are as much alike as any identical twins you're ever gonna meet.

When we stand together looking in the mirror, it's almost like we're two of those alien clones in horror movies (which we *love*).

I remember way back in sixth grade, we fooled *both* our homeroom teachers by switching places on April Fools' Day. We didn't get into trouble, but we did get called to the principal's office. Still, "the Fabulous Walker Twins" pulled the best April Fools' Day joke that school ever saw! We go to high school in New York City nowadays, but we have not been forgotten. I guess you can't blame them for never putting identical twins in the same class again after that!

Now that we have turned thirteen (our birthday is September 9, which makes us practical-minded Virgos), Angie and I don't always dress alike anymore—which makes it easier to tell us apart. But even when we do put on the same outfit, you can tell I'm Aquanette. I'm the one who's always running my mouth. Anginette is more the quiet type. But as Big Momma says, "She doesn't miss a trick."

Big Momma is our maternal grandmother, and she loves to brag about us—even to ladies in the supermarket! "I can't tell which one of them is smarter or cuter sometimes," she'll say. Or, "You know they've been singing like angels since they were cooing in the cradle."

That's not exactly true. I think we started singing when we were about three years old. Anyway, Big Momma says, "Singing is a gift from the Lord." Well, nobody else in our family can even hold a note, so it must be true.

And I *guess* we're kinda cute: Angie and I are both brown-skinned, with nice "juicy" lips and big brown eyes. Still, we're not *real* pretty, like the rest of the Cheetah Girls—that would be Galleria "Bubbles" Garibaldi, Chanel "Chuchie" Simmons, and Dorinda "Do' Re Mi" Rogers. That's right—Angie and I have only just moved to New York, and here we are, already in a singing group!

Angie and I met Galleria and Chanel at the Kats and Kittys Klub Fourth of July Bash last summer. It was right after we moved to New York from Houston, leaving Ma, Big Momma, and all our cousins behind. We woulda been real lost if it hadn't been for our fellow Kats and Kittys.

In case you've never heard of it, the Kats and Kittys Klub is this national organization for young, up-and-coming African Americans. They do lots of things for the community, and we used to go all the time back home. So we were real happy to join the metropolitan chapter in New York City, and that they were havin' a Fourth of July bar-b-que. It was our first chance to meet kids our own age in the Big Apple.

So there we were, singing up a storm by the barbecue grill, when Chanel and Galleria started looking at us *real* funny. I guess we were kinda showing off. They were the prettiest girls we had seen in New York, even though Galleria wasn't very friendly to us at first. Luckily, Chanel was, and now we're all *real* good friends and singing together.

We can't wait till Ma meets Galleria and the rest of the Cheetah Girls—which may not be anytime soon. See, she and Daddy are getting a dee-vorce, and Ma remained in Houston, while Daddy moved up here to New York.

Of course, Daddy sent for us to come live with him, so he could keep an eye on us. He feels that Ma can't properly supervise us. See, she's a regional district sales manager for Avon, and travels quite a bit for her job. Daddy used to be her boss, but you knew that wasn't gonna last long, because he can be *real* hard on people.

Even though he's *real* hard on us, too—making us do our vocal exercises and clean our rooms *every* night—we know he loves us. And we are real glad he let us invite our friends over here tonight.

That's right—he told us we could invite the Cheetah Girls over! This is the first time we've had company in New York. And the only reason Daddy said okay is because his new girlfriend came over, too.

Her name is High Priestess Abala Shaballa Bogo Hexagone, and believe it or not, she really is some kind of priestess from some far away place we never even heard of (even though we don't really know what a High Priestess is for sure). Angie and I don't like her much, but Daddy sure does. She's real tall and pretty, so I guess I can understand why.

Anyway, she came over today with her . . . well . . . friends, if that's what you want to call them. If you ask me, they are some of the strangest people you'd ever want to meet. And tonight, they're cookin' up some kind of spooky ritual for the Cheetah Girls!

I told my friends all about this at our last Cheetah Girls council meeting. But they thought I was just joking! Well, I wasn't, and they're about to find that out!

See, as a singing group, we've only performed together once—at the Cheetah-Rama club last Halloween night. It was a lot of fun! I think the Kats and Kittys liked us, and we got paid, too! We even got a manager out of it—but Mr. Jackal Johnson turned out to be a crook.

Still, even though we haven't performed much, we've got the biggest night of our lives coming up. Tomorrow night, the Cheetah Girls are performing at the world-famous Apollo Thee-ay-ter! Angie and I have never been there before, but we've seen it on television, so we know it's *real* big, with a lot of seats and bright lights and everything.

Don't get me wrong. We're just performing in the Apollo Theatre Amateur Hour contest—but we're still real nervous about it. Most of all, we're *real* scared about the Apollo Sandman. He is this kooky guy in a clown outfit who pulls you off the stage if people start booing at you!

So High Priestess Abala invited her friends over here to conduct this ritual to give the Cheetah Girls more "Growl Power." That's what she said. It sounds okay, till you get a good look at what they're doing back there in the kitchen. They're all standing around this table preparing stuff and jabbering something or other. And believe me, they are a weird collection of folks. I'll tell you, I don't know who I'm more scared of—the Sandman, or High Priestess Abala and her friends.

While they're all back there makin' their "witches' brew," Galleria is putting on a show in our living room. (Chanel and Dorinda are on their way over, too. They're just late.)

"Well, Miss *Aquanette* and *Anginette* Walker, that's downright plummy that you *finally* invited me to your house. Well, you Southern belles are just so swell!" Galleria says, fluttering her pretty eyelashes, and mocking Angie and me.

She loves to do that, and we think it's kinda funny, how she can find a way to rhyme almost anything. We know she's just playing with us, though, because we have a lot of fun together. There is nobody back home in Houston like Galleria Garibaldi. As Big Momma would say,

"They threw away the mold after they made her."

Next year, we hope Galleria and the rest of the Cheetah Girls are gonna transfer to *our* high school. See, they're freshmen at Fashion Industries High, but Angie and I go to LaGuardia High School of Performing Arts. It's very prestigious and all, so we're *real* lucky to be going there. We had to come to New York just for an audition, then go back home, all the way to Houston, and wait to see if we got accepted!

Angie and I just can't wait till the kids in our school see the Cheetah Girls singing together. They're gonna be so jealous—especially JuJu Beans Gonzalez, who's in our vocal and drama classes, and thinks she's the next Mo' Money Moniqe, just because she can rap and wiggle her shimmyshaker.

Angie and I don't dance *that* good, but still, we've got the shimmyshakers to do it, if we try real hard. That's all I'm saying. And we sing better than JuJu Beans does, even when we have colds (Angie and I always get sick together, too).

JuJu treats me and Angie like corn bread

bakers, or something "country" like that, just because she has never been to Houston. Houston is beautiful—even Galleria's mom, Ms. Dorothea, says so.

Anyway, we've got all year to convince our teachers to let us perform together as the Cheetah Girls for LaGuardia's big June talent showcase. We've been praying on it, and God always gives us an answer (even though most of the time it's not near as quick as we'd like!)

Galleria is acting like company. She sips her lemonade all dainty, then places the glass on its coaster on the coffee table—like it's Aladdin's lamp or something, and she's afraid all the wishes are gonna fly out of it!

Then she sits back on the couch with her legs tight together and her hands on her knees—just like some of the New York ladies sit in church (like they don't belong in the house of the Lord, or they don't know how they're supposed to sit in the pew).

"Dag on, Galleria, you don't have to be so proper. You can just be yourself," I heckle her, then throw Angie another glance. After all, we have seen the real Miss Galleria, and believe us, she does *just* as she pleases.

Now Galleria's eyes are moving around the living room like a pair of Ping-Pong balls. "Those drapes look like they belong in the Taj Mahal," she says, like she's amusing herself at a porch party down South, or something fancy like that.

The drapes *are* kinda nice, though. They're ivory chiffon, with a scarf valance that has fringes, just like the panels.

Daddy decorated the living room himself, right down to the plastic slipcovers—and he's real proud of it. The big glass coffee table has a brass lion base, and the only thing we're allowed to keep on top of the glass is a big white leather-bound Holy Bible. Then there's a big white shag rug shaped like a bear, lying in the center of the floor. The head has real ivory-looking fang teeth—we checked his mouth with a flashlight!

Daddy keeps his new snow globe collection in a big white wooden case with glass partitions. The snow globes are on the top shelves, and the bottom shelves are lined with his *precious* collection of LP albums—not CDs, but real records of people like Marvin Gaye, the Supremes, the Temptations. Daddy says he's invested too much in his record collection to start buying CDs now. When we were little, if we ever messed with Daddy's records, or broke one, he would get *real* mad at us.

"Holy cannoli, we got records like this too—but Momsy keeps them in storage, where they're just collecting dust!" Galleria says, laughing. "We could play Frisbee with one of these!"

She pretends to toss the vinyl record at me, but she knows better, because she's *real* careful putting it back into its jacket. Even *she* can tell Daddy is real particular about things. That's why he keeps the sofa and sectionals covered in plastic— "because the fabric is a very delicate imported ivory silk," he says. So nobody ends up sittin' on the couch but company.

Even Daddy, when he sits in the living room, sits in the big brown leather reclining chair—so he can watch the big television, which is behind a set of wooden panels. The couch just sits there, showin' off, "no use to nobody," as Big Momma used to say. But this is Daddy's house now, and he decorates it like he pleases.

One thing is for sure—our house in New York (we call it a house even though it's just a two-bedroom duplex apartment) is decorated *real* different from the way Ma decorated our house in Houston. Daddy likes everything to be white, ivory, or brown, which are *his* favorite colors. Ma liked peach, and green, and blue colors.

Before I start making myself jittery again—about tonight *and* tomorrow night—the doorbell rings. Thank God, it's finally Chanel and Dorinda. After quick kisses and hugs, Chanel becomes fascinated with our house too.

"Ooh, *qué bonita*! My abuela Florita would love these," she coos, pointing to Daddy's prized collection of snow globes. (That's her grandma she's talkin' about. That's how they say it in Spanish.)

"Abuela just loves the snow here. She'll go outside on her stoop and sit there all day, waiting for snowflakes to hit her on the nose!" Chanel takes the castle snow globe and shakes it up and down, to see the snow fall.

"Daddy just started collecting those. It's really kinda strange," I explain, my voice trailing off as I start to think how much Daddy has changed since he moved up here to New York.

"Aqua, what's wrong with collecting snow globes?" Dorinda asks.

Galleria has finally jumped up from the couch, now that Chanel and Dorinda are here. "Your *daddy's* probably fascinated by the snow we have here in 'New Yawk,'" she says with a laugh. "Wait till he experiences his first snowstorm—he'll be throwing those things out the window!

"My dad used to love the snow," she goes on. "When I was little, he would get more upset than I did if it didn't snow before Christmas. Then we had that majordomo snowstorm a few years ago, and it completely covered my Dad's van. He sat at the window for three days, cursing in Italian till he could shovel his van out!"

"It's not just the snow globes, *Galleria*," I say, exasperated. "That was only the beginning. Then he bought a blender—"

"What's wrong with a blender?" Chanel asks.

"Now everything he eats comes outta that thing!" I say, exasperated.

Chanel bursts out laughing, which makes Galleria and even Dorinda smirk.

"I wish *I* had a blender," Dorinda says,

narrowing her eyes at me, which almost makes her look like a real cheetah. "Where I live, I've got to chop up all the vegetables by hand." Dorinda lives in an apartment with about ten foster brothers and sisters. Bless her heart. I wouldn't trade with her for nothing in the world. Lucky for her, her foster mother just adopted her—so at least she knows she can keep on living where she is, instead of going to another foster home.

Galleria is still riffing about Daddy's blender. "Oh, snapples, he blended apples, and now Aqua thinks he's gonna turn into Freddy!" Galleria snaps, doing the Cheetah Girl handshake with Chanel.

"What Aqua means, is—" Angie says, coming to my defense, "he used to love to cook, you know? Cajun crawfish—"

"—Steaks smothered in onions and gravy," I chime in, so they understand that our Daddy used to like to *eat*. "Now he's blending strange vegetables and fruits, and he sits there and drinks it, like it's supposed to be dee-licious."

"And he expects *us* to drink those dees-gusting shakes too!" Angie cuts in.

"I mean, celery and turnip shakes—please, where's Mikki D's?" I say, rolling my eyes. My friends start laughing again, because they know *we* love to eat, too.

"Snow globes, a stupid blender, and now *this*," I say, pointing to the kitchen, where Daddy is standing with his new girlfriend and those other strange ladies she brought with her.

"What's her name again?" Chanel asks, pulling on one of her braids.

"High Priestess Abala Shaballa Bogo Hexagone,"I tell her. "She says she is a Hexagone High Priestess, and her ancestors reigned in Ancient Hexagonia." I roll my eyes like I can't believe it myself.

"Is a Hexagone High Priestess supposed to be like Nefertiti or someone like that?" Dorinda asks, narrowing her eyes again. She knows about all kinds of stuff, because she reads a whole lot of books.

"I don't think so, 'cuz this 'High Priestess' has definitely got a broomstick parked around the corner! Right, Angie?"

"I think High Priestess is just a fancy name for *witch*!" Angie answers.

"*Parate*, Aqua," Chanel says, bursting into giggles. "Help, you're killing me—maybe she's a good witch, *mija*?"

"Well, I don't know, but I'm glad y'all are here, because the show is about to begin! Right before Galleria came, they went to the Piggly Wiggly Supermarket to buy ingredients—'for the ritual!' they said!"

Finally, Galleria and Chanel aren't laughing anymore. Now they're sitting on the edge of their seats, like they're about to see a horror movie. And, believe me, I think we are!

Chapter 2

Suddenly, we hear a loud, grinding noise coming from the kitchen.

"You hear that?" I ask, my eyes popping open.

"*Sí*," Chanel responds.

"That's the blender going—see?" Angie says, her eyes getting wide.

"You know, you and Angie do the same things with your eyes," Chanel says to me, bugging her eyes wide and imitating us.

"I'll bet you they're blending the witches' brew for us to drink!" I whisper.

"That's it—I'm outtie like Snouty," Dorinda says, crossing her arms and looking at Chanel.

"What's that you said, Dorinda?" I ask

politely. Sometimes, when Galleria, Dorinda, and Chanel talk, Angie and I don't understand them. I mean, everybody in New York talks so fast—but our friends just have their *own* way of talking.

Angie says we shouldn't ask when we don't understand what they say, because it makes us look stupid. But as Big Momma always says, "If you don't ask, you gonna miss a whole lot of conversation!"

"It means, Aqua, that I'd rather go get a soda and some chips at the Piggy Wiggly Supermarket than sit here and wait to get hit over the head with a broomstick!" Dorinda grunts, then sits up straight on the couch and folds her arms across her little chest.

Oh, *I* get what she means. She's talking about the snout on the plastic pig outside of Piggly Wiggly. That Dorinda is so cute. She sure can eat, for someone so little. She must have had three slices of our sweet potato pie at her surprise adoption party. (We made it from scratch, too. Not like those store-bought winky-dinky pies and cakes that people serve their families here. Shame on them!)

"Do' Re Mi, why you trying to flounce, when

we know you wuz 'bout to bounce?" Galleria says in her singing voice. "That's why I'm writing my new song about you. You're always trying to bounce!"

Dorinda just sits with her arms folded, looking *real* sheepish, but Galleria lets her off the hook. See, Galleria wrote a new song about Dorinda, because she almost left the group when she got offered a job as a backup dancer for the Mo' Money Monique tour. Do' Re Mi turned the job down in the end, 'cuz she wanted to stay with all of us. But I guess Galleria and Chanel are still sore about it, since they were the ones who made Dorinda a Cheetah Girl in the first place.

"It's time to 'winter squash' this situation, if you know what I'm saying," Galleria says, laughing. "Let's go in the kitchen and blend us a High Priestess Abala shake!" She jumps up, like she's gonna march into the kitchen herself. We all start giggling.

"Dorinda's 'bout to bounce!" Chanel sings, and we all sing a call-and-response verse:

"Who's trying to flounce?"

"Dorinda! Dorinda!"

When we finish singing, I ask, kinda

nervous, "Do you all understand *why* we're waiting for Abala and her friends?" I'm not quite sure how to get through to them.

"No, why?" Chanel asks, sipping her lemonade. One of her braids accidentally dips in the glass, and she starts to giggle nervously. "Oops, *Lo siento*. I didn't see the glass coming!"

"Y'all better listen to what I'm sayin', Chanel," I continue, "and all the rest of you, too! The High Priestess Abala Shaballa says she wants to put a 'Vampire Spell' on us—so we'll captivate the audience at the Apollo Theatre tomorrow night."

The living room gets *real* quiet. It's so quiet, if you listen real close, you can probably hear the fake confetti snowflakes swirling around in Daddy's snow globes in the showcase.

"A 'Vampire Spell'?" Dorinda repeats, narrowing her eyes like a cheetah cub ready to pounce on its prey. "How do you spell, 'I'm outtie like Snouty'?"

She jumps up, but Galleria pushes her down. "Aqua, how could you have us come over here? This is not just some guy jumping out of his coffin and chasing us with his fake rubber arm, like at the haunted house in Madison 'Scare' Garden. This is *for real*!"

"Dag on!" I say. "I told you all during the Cheetah Girl council meeting this was *serious*." Looking at my hands in my lap, I try to figure out what to say to get the Cheetah Girls to help me and Angie. *God, give me the words.*

"What do you expect us to do? Stay here by ourselves, and let these people turn us into frogs instead of Cheetah Girls?"

"Aqua is right," Angie says, speaking up for me. "Then what are y'all gonna do without us? Aqua and I can't exactly go on stage hopping around and croaking, can we?" Angie folds her arms, like that's supposed to really make them help us, but all they do is start laughing.

I'm thinking this whole thing is a lost cause, but when they finish their latest round of giggles, Galleria quips, "Okay, we'll stay. But after this, you owe us, so don't snow us, Aqua." She turns, and looks at Chanel and Dorinda for backup.

"Dag on, all right, we owe y'all, Galleria," I say, giving in. "We're crew now, like you said, right?"

"Yeah," Galleria says, looking at me like, *what's your point?*

"Well then, we have to help each other out no matter what, right?" I continue.

"Yeah, but like I said before, after this you owe us, so don't snow us." When Galleria gets that tone in her voice, we know that's the final word—like she's Reverend Butter at church!

Angie cuts us a quick look, to tell us that Daddy is coming this way. We just sit *real* tight and wait for the fright show to begin.

"Hello, ladies," Daddy greets my friends. Right behind him are High Priestess Abala Shaballa and her coven of witches pretending to be normal ladies.

Abala is real dark—darker than *us*—and it makes her teeth look real white. She is real pretty, though, and she wears African fabric draped around her body and head.

Her friends, on the other hand, are real strange-looking. They trail into the living room, with their long gowns sweeping the floor, and their arms full of all kinds of what look to be witchcraft things. One of them is this dwarf lady, carrying the little folding table Daddy uses when he eats in front of the television.

"Good evening, ladies," High Priestess Abala Shaballa Bogo Hexagone says in a booming voice. "All blessings to Great Hexagone, and the bounty she has prepared for us this evening." Abala Shaballa stretches out her arms to us.

I give Daddy a look, like, I hope you know what you're doing. But what I'm really thinking is, How could you do this to us?

"The Piggly Wiggly Supermarket here is *divine*," says the dwarf lady, in a squeaky voice that sounds like the Tin Man in a rainstorm! "Ah, I see your friends have arrived. I'm Rasputina Twia."

"I'm Hecate Sukoji," says a woman with long black hair and no eyebrows. I wonder, did she shave off her eyebrows, or was she born that way?

"I'm Bast Bojo," says the third lady. She has a bald head, and is looking at us with beady eyes that are so dark and slanty, she looks like a spooky black cat!

"Let us begin," High Priestess Abala Shaballa says.

Rasputina puts down the folding table. On top of it, High Priestess Abala and her three friends put a goose, some tomatoes, beets, Tabasco sauce—

Now, wait a minute! I know Daddy is not

gonna let us use *that*. He always says hot sauce is bad for our vocal chords! But he's just smiling proudly, looking on.

I know—she probably already put a spell on Daddy! *And now we're next*!

Bast pulls some strange-looking fruits out of her pockets. "These are kumquats," she says, as if reading our minds. Then she pulls out a head of lettuce and a teddy bear from the basket she's carrying. Well, at least our pet guinea pigs Porgy and Bess will have something to eat for later—the lettuce, that is.

"You got that at Piggly Wiggly?" I ask in disbelief, looking at the raggedy teddy bear. *What on earth are they gonna do with a teddy bear, anyway*?

"Yes. Apparently it was left over from last Christmas," Rasputina says, all proud of herself.

High Priestess Abala kisses the garlic necklace around her neck. Then she pours some Tabasco sauce into the witches' brew in the blender, shakes it a little, and pours it out into five big glasses!

"Now, let us stand in a circle and drink up, Cheetah Girls, so that tomorrow night, when you're out for blood on the stage, you'll be able to hold your ground!" The High Priestess gives us a big, scary smile.

"What's in this, um, brew?" Dorinda asks, kinda nervous. Good for her. At least she has the nerve to speak up! Daddy must be in a trance or something!

"Raw steak, beets, tomatoes . . . I added pimientos, Tabasco, and, um . . . other things, to prepare you for battle!" High Priestess Abala smiles again, revealing her big, white teeth.

Sniffing at my glass, I think, I'll bet she put blood in it, too!

"Drink up," Abala commands, watching me closely. I drink the dag on thing—which to my surprise, actually tastes kinda good.

"Excellent! And now the rest of you! Come, drink up, girls!" Abala commands.

After we all drink the brew, we hold hands. "We must finish the ritual by paying homage to the sylphs of the east, the salamanders of the south, the bats of the west, and the gnomes of the north," Abala says, her voice sounding stranger and stranger.

At the end of the ritual, Abala gives each of us a shoe box. "You must not open these," she tells us. "Just put them in your closets, and close the door."

"What's in here?" Galleria asks, trying to hide a smirk.

"Parts from stuffed animals—teddy bear eyes and noses, poodle tails, rabbit whiskers . . ."

The High Priestess looks Galleria right in the eye, and Bubbles seems to shrink. "After midnight, the teddy bear, poodle, and rabbit will merge with you, and give you the strength of a true Cheetah Girl!"

"Oh," says Galleria, still smirking. "Well, I guess I'd better let my dog Toto know we'll be having company later—I wouldn't want 'Mr. Teddy Poodly' to get his nose bitten off when he comes out to play."

We all start laughing. High Priestess Abala just looks at us, amused. I wonder what's going through her mind. I don't like all this one bit, I'll tell you that!

Angie and I are gonna do some real praying tonight—and I'm gonna Scotch-tape our shoe boxes so tight, even the Mummy himself wouldn't be able to get out of them!

That High Priestess may have Daddy under a spell, but she doesn't fool me. Tonight, I'm gonna ask *God* to please help us win the Apollo Theatre Amateur Hour Contest—and not to let High Priestess Abala Shaballa turn Daddy into a salamander!

Chapter 3

Mr. Garibaldi wanted to drive us Cheetah Girls to the Apollo Theatre tonight, but Daddy insisted that *he* drive us. It made us feel *real* important to have everybody fussing over us, like we're a big singing group already, with cheetah-licious ways.

Daddy has two cars—a white Cadillac with a convertible top, and a white Bronco—and, can you believe this? He has to *pay* to keep them in a garage near our house!

He's always fussin' about that. Back home we had three cars—including the blue Katmobile, which is now Ma's—*and* our own four-car garage in the back of the house. And we didn't have to pay a dime extra for all that parking space! I'll tell you, New York City sure is strange—and expensive. I'm surprised they don't charge for breathing air here!

Anyway, Daddy *insisted* that Mr. Garibaldi and Ms. Dorothea drive with us to the Apollo. (Chanel's mom is out on a big date with her boyfriend, Mr. Tycoon, so she can't come see us tonight. She's tryin' to get Mr. Tycoon to marry her, but he's playin' hard to get, so *she's* taking belly dancing lessons to "get" *him*!)

Ms. Dorothea doesn't like us to call her Mrs. Garibaldi, because she isn't a "prim and proper" kind of person. If you met her, you would understand where Galleria gets all her personality. I mean, Galleria is tame compared to her mother—Ms. Dorothea even eats Godiva chocolates for breakfast, and hits people over the head with her Cheetah pocketbook when they're acting up. We just love her! By putting up the two extra seats in the back of Daddy's Bronco, we're all able to fit. Since Dorinda and Chanel are the smallest, they sit on the two little seats way in the back. Galleria sits next to her mom and dad.

We're *so* glad High Priestess Abala Shaballa couldn't come with us tonight to the Apollo

Theatre, even though she says she is "with us in the spirit." Well, I keep looking out the car window to make sure I don't see her in the *flesh*, flying by on her broomstick with her flock of kooky friends! (So far, the coast is clear.) I'm sorry, but Angie and I decided last night that we don't trust "High Priestess Hocus Pocus," as Galleria calls her.

"Angie, would you look at all these people?" I say, as we drive across 125th Street. It seems like there are millions of people in New York, and they are *all* walking around up here in Harlem. I mean, the sidewalks are so crowded, it looks like they're having a fair or something!

"*Mira,* look at their outfits. Some of them look like they're dressed for church!" Chanel exclaims.

"What church is *she* going to in a yellow satin cape?" Dorinda chides Chanel, pointing to a lady whose earrings are so big, they look like plates hanging from her ears. Girls in New York just *love* their jewelry.

"Well, you never know—this is the Big Apple," Angie chimes in.

"I know. I've never seen so many neon signs before in my life!" I say.

Dorinda points to a hair-supply place with a giant neon sign that says RAPUNZEL. "Word, that's the hair place Abiola at the YMCA told me about!"

Dorinda has a *real* after-school job—through the youth entrepreneurship program at the YMCA—even though it doesn't pay that much. "That's where we should buy hair, so we don't look like wefties!" she adds, chuckling. Wefties are girls with weaves that are so tick tacky the tracks are showing, as Galleria says.

"*Mamacitas*, they've got some hefty wefties up here," Chanel says, looking at more girls walking by in their fancy outfits. "They must be going to some kinda club around here."

"Yeah—a club for vampires!" exclaims Galleria, as we pass the Black Magic movie-theater complex. "Ooo, look, Aqua and Angie, they're having a Fang-oria Festival there!"

From what I can see, the Black Magic looks big enough to fit all the people in New York *and* Houston. "Let's go see Freddy before we get ready!" I say excitedly.

"Hmmph—then Freddy will have to deal with me, because no ghoul is gonna stop this show!" Ms. Dorothea quips, then yawns into her leopard-gloved hand.

"Gee, Momsy poo, I think the Sandman has already sprinkled you with some poppy dust or something," Galleria giggles.

"I'm fading *pronto,* too," says Mr. Garibaldi, who is also yawning. "I get up every day at five o'clock, you know."

"Before the rooster can say cock-a-doodle-do!" Galleria chides her father.

Ms. Dorothea is getting up early too these days. She's working *real* hard now that she is our manager, and she still runs her fancy boutique—Toto in New York . . . Fun in Diva Sizes—which is the most beautiful store I've ever seen.

"Ooh, they got *Blacula* there! We've never seen that one!" Angie says to me, getting real excited. We just love horror movies—especially the old ones, because they show more gory stuff up close, like eyeballs hanging out of the eye sockets, or brains popping out of the skull.

The only thing I love more than singing is looking at dead bodies, and figuring out how they died, and wondering if they'll tell any secrets. I guess that's because our Granddaddy

Walker is a mortician and owns "Rest in Peace," the biggest funeral parlor in Houston.

Over the last forty years, Granddaddy Walker has buried half of the dead people in Houston. That's what Big Momma says.

When our singing career is over, I'm going to become a forensic scientist, like that guy on the old TV show—you know, the one who solves crimes by examining the victims. Angie wants to be a neurosurgeon, so she can operate on people's brains and stuff.

I'm so scared, I wish we could see a horror movie right now. When Daddy gets out of the car to find out where he should park, we all start cackling about last night's strange events.

"Did any of y'all dance with a teddy bear or a poodle last night?" I ask. Then I wonder, What on earth did Abala mean by giving us stuffed teddy bear heads in a shoe box? How was that supposed to help us win this competition?

"I couldn't believe Aqua got up in the morning and checked our shoe boxes in the closet, just to make sure they were still taped," Angie says, acting all grown.

"Angie, don't act like *you* didn't look at your box, too," I shoot back.

"Can you believe Abala says Galleria was probably Egyptian royalty in her past life?" Dorinda remarks, still in disbelief about last night.

"Well, she's definitely not psychic, or she would know that we don't like her!" I say, huffing and puffing. Angie and I are squeezed into the front seat, and we're trying not to breathe, so we don't bust out of our Cheetah Girls costumes.

"I'm gonna ask Princess Pamela about her, *para seguro,*" Chanel says. "Just to be safe. You can count on that, *está bien?*"

Like I said before, Princess Pamela is Chanel's father's girlfriend. Chuchie's parents have been divorced for a while, and she just loves Pamela. The Princess owns a whole lot of businesses—she does hair and nails, bakes the best pound-cake in New York, and tells people's fortunes. Princess Pamela is a psychic. She may not be a High Priestess like Abala, but I like Pamela a lot better. *She* can tell *my* fortune any time.

"I think my jumpsuit is tighter than it was the last time," I say.

"Those sweet potato pies you made for Dorinda's surprise adoption party were dope-a-licious, but did you have to eat five of them all by yourself, Miz Aquanette?" Galleria asks, laying on that syrupy Southern accent again.

"No, I guess not, Miz Galleria," I sigh back, playing along with her. "And I guess it didn't help that I ate all of your father's chocolate cannolis at the same time!"

"Aah, *mama mia*, I wondered who ate them all!" Mr. Garibaldi says, waving his hand.

I take another deep breath. I'm scared I'm gonna pop out of my costume right on stage, and the Sandman is gonna tear the rest of my costume with his big ol' hook!

Now I feel like poor Dorinda did when she tore her costume onstage at the Cheetah-Rama. You should have seen her face when she ripped her jumpsuit. That's right—there we were, in the middle of a song—and Dorinda did a lickety-split, right there on stage!

"Don't worry, Aqua. You won't be a witch without a stitch," says Galleria, leaning from the back of the car and whispering in my ear. "And it's just a matter of time before we pull the curtain on the High Priestess of Hocus Pocus. The Wizard of Oz she ain't, or I'll faint!"

"What does she do when she isn't concocting Vampire Spells?" Dorinda asks.

"Daddy says she teaches this, well . . . witchcraft stuff to people. And she has a store called Enchantrixx up here somewhere."

Then I see Daddy on his way back to the car. "Shh, he's coming," I whisper, then announce loudly as he opens the door, "Well! Here we are at the world-famous Apollo Theatre."

Mentioning the Apollo reminds me of why we're here tonight, and how much is at stake. It makes me start feeling nervous, and when I get nervous, my stomach starts churning like it's mashing potatoes or something.

"Y'all feeling scared like I am?" I ask, this time turning around so I can look at Galleria.

"Sí, mamacita," admits Chanel.

"I guess that's natural, right?" Dorinda asks Ms. Dorothea. Ever since the adoption party, the two of them seem like two peas in a pod—which we're all *real* happy about.

Dorinda needs all the love she can get. She's been a foster child all her life—till now, that is. The day her foster mother, Mrs. Bosco, adopted her was the best day of Dorinda's whole life. It sure made Ms. Dorothea cry a lot, though. I wonder what that was all about. She seemed *so* sad about something.

"Darling, when the day comes that you're not afraid as you walk on that stage—cancel the show immediately!" Dorothea says, reaching for the door handle to get out.

But Mr. Garibaldi quickly says, "*Cara*, no, let me get the door for you!"

Mr. Garibaldi is such a gentleman. Galleria says he's very "old school," because he grew up in Italy and not here in the States.

That's probably true. When we were at Ms. Dorothea's store, Galleria showed us the personals ad from *New York* magazine that Ms. Dorothea answered to meet Mr. Garibaldi. We almost died right there on the spot! He called himself a "lonely oyster on the half shell" in the ad. I can't imagine him like that. He seems like the happiest man we've ever seen. We wish Daddy was more like that—just a lot of fun, that's all I'm saying.

After Mr. Garibaldi helps all of us out of the car, we take a look up at the sign for the Apollo Theatre. "Look at all the lights up there!" I exclaim.

"They should have *our* name up there in bright lights, taking up the whole marquee!" Galleria says, giggling.

"Darling, one day they *will*," Ms. Dorothea says, then flings her fur boa around her neck, which hits Mr. Garibaldi in the face.

"Don't knock me out with your love, *cara*!" he quips, then puts the boa back on her shoulder.

We are giggling up a storm, because we are just so happy to be here. People are looking at us as we walk in, and Ms. Dorothea tells the usher that we're The Cheetah Girls and we're here to *perform*.

"Go right in, ladies," the usher says, smiling at us. He looks so nice in his uniform. He's wearing a red jacket, black pants and white gloves—and his teeth are almost as bright as the neon lights in the sign!

As we're walking by all the people waiting to buy popcorn and stuff at the concession stand, these two tall, skinny guys with baseball caps and real baggy pants start calling to us. "You're grrrr-eat! Yo, check it, D, there's Tony the Tiger with his girlfriends!" They stand there stuffing popcorn in their mouths, and heckling up a storm. They are so loud that everybody turns and looks at us.

"Well if it isn't the baggy, bumbling Bozo brothers, trying to get full at the concession stand!" Galleria hisses back.

"Shhh, darling, never let them see you sweat," Ms. Dorothea tells her. "Besides, those children look like they could use a home-cooked meal."

It's still so hard for me and Angie to believe how rude people in New York can be. I mean, we have *some* "bozos" in Houston, but not like this. People will just walk up to you anywhere and get in your face, for no reason!

"Dag on, I hope everybody ain't like him, or this is gonna turn into a 'Nightmare on 125th Street,'" I turn and say to Galleria. (One of my favorite horror movies is *Nightmare on Elm Street*, 'cuz that scar-faced Freddy Krueger always finds a way to get in your dreams and scare you to death!)

"Not to worry, Aqua. There is always one sour bozo in a bunch of grapes!" Galleria mutters.

"Let's find our dressing room," quips Ms. Dorothea, acting now like our manager—which is what she *has* been, ever since she helped us get rid of that no-good Mr. Jackal Johnson.

"Darling, I'll see you later," Mr. Garibaldi says, kissing Ms. Dorothea on the cheek. Then he says good-bye to us, so he can find some seats up front for himself and Daddy.

"Try to sit in the first row, Daddy!" Galleria yells back to him, as we walk toward the back.

Ms. Dorothea speaks to another usher in a red jacket who points straight ahead of us. "Right that way, ladies."

"Look at all the people!" Chanel says excitedly. Lots of them are already filing into the theater and finding their seats.

"It *is* as big as it looks on TV!" I whisper to Angie.

"You think it'll get filled up?" Dorinda asks, kinda nervous.

"Sí, sí, Do' Re Mi," says Chanel, giggling. "As soon as they find out *we're* here, *está bien?"*

At the base of the stairs, there is a woman with a walkie-talkie and earphones. Before Ms. Dorothea says anything to her, the woman tells us in a brisk voice to "go up the stairs."

Dag on! She could be a little friendlier, I think to myself, as we all climb up a real tiny staircase. It seems like the longest time before we get to the stairwell landing for dressing room "B."

When we open the stairwell door, there are a lot of people crowded in the hallway! *Are we supposed to share a dressing room with all these people*? I wonder.

"Excuse me, darlings," Ms. Dorothea says firmly, pushing her way through the throng of people.

"You'd think we were at the mall or something, and they were giving things away!" Angie exclaims.

As we pour into the dressing room, just to plop down our things, Ms. Dorothea quips, "They said the dressing room would be small, but this looks like a *prison cell*!"

"I guess it's a good thing we already have our costumes on," I say nervously, looking around at the other people. They are in costumes too, but not like ours. One man looks just like The Cat In the Hat or something, his hat is so high up on his head. He has striped kneesocks, too, and shorts, and big cartoon-looking glasses!

Galleria whispers, "If all we've got to deal

with is The Cat In the Hat, then we've got it made, like green eggs and ham!"

I sure hope so, I think nervously—because between my too tight costume, this too tight dressing room, and High Priestess Abala's too spooky Vampire Spell, this whole thing is turning into a New York frightmare!

Chapter 4

"I bet Dressing Room 'A' is for the stars," Dorinda says, looking kinda sad, then puts her cheetah backpack down on the floor.

"What *stars*, darling?" Ms. Dorothea says. "In my humble opinion, you girls are the most cheetah-licious thing the Apollo Theatre has ever seen—or will ever see!"

We may not exactly believe her, but at least her words make us feel less nervous. Now we have to push through the people again, and climb all the way back down those steep little stairs until we get backstage. *Then* we have to wait backstage for our number to be called.

"I'm exhausted already!" I moan to Dorinda, who is scratching herself through her costume.

Oh, no, not again. She can't be busting out of her costume, after Ms. Dorothea took all that time to fix it!

As if reading my mind, Dorinda squints her eyes and says, "Don't worry, Aqua, my costume is not gonna rip again. I must have got bitten by mosquitoes or *something* last night. Our screens at the house have holes in them."

"Maybe it was the little teddy bear vampire from your shoe box!" Galleria says, her eyes lighting up.

"Lemme see," Chanel says to Do' Re Mi, who rolls up the left leg on her cheetah jumpsuit. "*Ay, Dios!* Look how red they are. *Mamacita,* it sure looks like mosquito bites to me."

"Maybe you got bitten by those mosquitoes carrying the killer virus!" Galleria says, concerned.

"Maybe it was one of those six-foot bloodsucking mosquitoes like in the movie me and Aqua saw," my twin blurts out.

"I'm not trying to hear this," Dorinda says, getting upset.

"Don't worry, Dorinda. I know how to stop the itching," I say.

"How, brown cow?" Bubbles asks, giggling.

"Darling, that's not funny," Ms. Dorothea says suddenly.

"What, Mom? I'm just riffing off a *nursery* rhyme!" Galleria protests.

"Even so, darling, sometimes you have to give your 'riff' the 'sniff test' before you 'flap your lips'—if you 'get my drift,'" Ms. Dorothea says, looking at Galleria like she's not the only one with rhyme power.

Galleria gets real sheepish. Ms. Dorothea is real nice, but she doesn't play.

"That's all right, Ms. Dorothea, I know Galleria didn't mean anything bad. She's just being, well, herself," I offer as an explanation.

"Well, she can stir that saying with some jam, and make *flim-flam*," Ms. Dorothea says, closing her cheetah purse with a loud snap.

We all get quiet, but I don't want Galleria to feel bad, so I say, "I can go upstairs and get the deodorant out of my backpack."

"For what, *mamacita*? You trying to say we smell now?" Chanel asks me.

"No, Chanel! It's an old Southern remedy. If you rub deodorant on a mosquito bite, it stops the itching!"

"Word?" Dorinda asks hopefully.

"Well then, go get it, Aqua, 'cuz we don't want Dorinda wiggling around like Mr. Teddy Poodly onstage," Galleria says, making a joke about the stuffed teddy bear head and poodle tail in the shoe boxes Abala gave us.

"Dag on, I hope that thing doesn't try on any of my clothes while I'm gone!" I retort. That gets everyone laughing, which is good, because we don't want to get a bad case of nerves before we perform.

"I'll go with you, Aqua," Ms. Dorothea says. "You girls stay here, so nobody takes our spot." She looks annoyed. "Of course, at the rate they're going, we'll be here until the Cock-a-doodle Donut truck pulls up to make a morning delivery!"

When we get back upstairs, I can't believe that those bozo boys we met when we came in are hanging out near our dressing room. They're putting on yellow satin jackets, with the words "Stak Chedda" written on the back in blue letters. That must be the name of their group, I figure.

I grab the deodorant for Dorinda and we head back downstairs. "I bet they're probably rappers," I say to Ms. Dorothea, once we're safely out of hearing range.

"Like I said, darling, that is still no excuse for bad manners!" Dorothea quips.

When we get backstage and rejoin the others, I give Do' Re Mi the deodorant for her legs, and she starts working on herself.

"Guess who's performing!" I moan. "Those bozos we met outsi—"

Galleria jabs me before I can finish, so I turn around. Can you believe it? Those rude boys are coming our way!

"Whazzup, ladies?" the one with the Popeye eye sockets says to us, chuckling under his breath.

"Are you performing too?" Dorinda asks. Galleria is propping her up while Angie puts the deodorant on the mosquito bites on her leg.

"Yeah. We're rappers—'Stak Chedda.' I'm Stak Jackson and this is my brother Chedda Jackson," Popeye says to us.

"Who are you lovely ladies?" Chedda asks. His head is bigger than his brother's, but the rest of his body still looks like he could use a home-cooked meal—just like Ms. Dorothea said.

"We're the Cheetah Girls," Galleria answers for us, then gives them a smirk, like, "don't try it."

"See? I knew y'all were related to Tony the Tiger!" Popeye riffs. "Those costumes you're wearing are fierce, though."

"They're not costumes—it's our survival gear for becoming stars in the jiggy jungle—not wanna-be's like you." Galleria sniffs, then adds, "And you two must be related to Dr. Jekyll and Mr. Hyde?"

"Oooops," Chedda says, then slaps his baseball cap at the crown.

"I mean the rappers, not the loony doctors," Galleria assures them. "But maybe . . ."

"We could have it like that. You never know, with how we flow," Popeye says, then slaps his brother a high five.

"It's show time at the Apollo!" booms the announcer's voice from the front of the stage. Then we hear loud applause.

"It's crowded out there, right?" says one of the girls in back of us, really loudly.

"Quiet, please, and keep your places, so you can be called on," says an attendant with a walkie-talkie.

When the girls in back of us keep yapping, Ms. Dorothea gives them a look, then says, "Shhh!" Then she huddles the five of us together in a circle. "It's time to do your Cheetah Girls prayer."

Even though the area backstage is small and crowded with all the contestants, we try to ignore everybody and do our Cheetah Girls prayer. We have plenty of time, because we're the fourth contestants—even though I wish we were the last, because I'm starting to feel real nervous. The hamburger I ate for dinner is churning around in my stomach.

Ms. Dorothea instructs us to join hands, bow our heads, and close our eyes. Galleria starts the prayer; then we join in, keeping our voices low, so the other people around us don't start looking at us.

"Dear Head Cheetah in Charge, please give us the growl power to perform our cheetah-licious best, and make you proud of all the gifts you've bestowed on us . . ." We end the prayer by doing the Cheetah Girl handshake together and chanting, "Whatever makes us clever—forever!"

The other people backstage cheer us on

quietly. But they don't have to worry—there is so much noise coming from the stage and the audience, you can't even hear us back here.

"Bacon, Once Over Lightly—please stand here by the curtain. You go on first," the attendant barks sharply. She is talking to four girls who look a lot older than us—maybe about nineteen—and are wearing brown leather jumpers and kneesocks.

"I hope they're crispy," whispers Galleria, who is standing between me and Chanel.

"Their earrings sure look like plates—big enough to hold a few strips," I whisper back.

"Ladies and gentleman," booms the announcer, "we've got four sisters from Buttercup, Tennessee. Let's give a hand to Bacon, Once Over Lightly!"

Sisters. They must not be sisters for real, 'cuz they don't look very much alike. Maybe that's just a stage act or something. We hold our breath, waiting for the girls to start singing.

First we hear the track for the Sista Fudge song, "I'll Slice You Like a Poundcake," booming on the sound system. They'd better be real good singers to mess with that song, I think, shaking my head.

Pulling down my jumpsuit, Galleria slaps my hand and mouths, "Stop it!" but I don't even care, 'cuz I can't believe my ears. These poor girls are more like Spam than bacon—they sound like the noise from an electric can opener!

All of a sudden, the noise from the audience is even louder than their singing.

"Omigod—are they booing them?" Angie asks, bobbing her head around to see if maybe she can sneak a peek through the curtain. But we can't see a thing. The attendant is standing right near the heavy curtain, and it's not budging.

Suddenly I start sweating. There is no air back here. It's hot, and I'm nervous. Those girls are getting booed out there! Are *we* gonna get booed too? I can't believe how blasé the attendant is acting! She must be used to all this.

"I think they're awright. They didn't have to boo them like that," Dorinda says, folding her arms. Her lower lip is kinda trembling, and I can tell she feels sorry for Bacon, Once Over Lightly. Ms. Dorothea puts her arms around Dorinda's little shoulders and gives her a squeeze.

All of a sudden, we hear this funny music, and the audience laughing real loud. We just look at each other, like, "Where's Freddy?"

"That means the Sandman went onstage," Ms. Dorothea tells us.

That really did sound like *clown* music or something. I have to catch my breath and say a prayer to God. *Please give us the strength to perform after all this. And please don't let the Sandman take us!*

Then I get the strangest thought: What if High Priestess Abala Shaballa *did* put a spell on us? What if we go out there and start croaking like bullfrogs?

No! That's so silly! We had rehearsal today, and we sound just as good as we always do. And at least we're singing original material, I remind myself. Galleria writes songs—she's *real* talented like that, even if we did fight in the beginning 'cuz she likes to have everything her way.

She wrote the song we're singing tonight, "Wanna-be Stars in the Jiggy Jungle." When we performed it for the first time at the Cheetah-Rama, everybody *loved* it!

They'll probably love us tonight, too. That's right, I tell myself. Angie and I look at each other, and I know she's thinking the same thing.

Two more acts go on—the Coconuts and a boy named Wesley Washington, who tries to sing falsetto like Jiggie Jim from the Moonpies, one of my favorite singers. (He just gives me goose bumps, his voice is so high and beautiful.) This boy sounds like he has been inhaling helium or something. He is definitely singing too high for his range.

"I think we're the only ones singing an original song," I whisper in Galleria's ear.

She pokes me in the stomach and says, "No diggity, no doubt!"

Now it's our turn. The walkie-talkie attendant motions for us to hurry up and stand by her.

I whisper to Chanel, "Ain't you scared? We don't know what's waiting for us beyond that curtain!"

"Fame!" giggles Chanel, grabbing my hand.

"Ladies and gentleman, our next contestants are five young ladies from right here in the Big Apple, and they got a whole lot of attitude!"

How come he didn't say two of us are from Houston? I feel kinda mad, but I just smile when he says, "Give it up for the Cheetah

Girls!" What counts is, he got the name of our group right.

We run out onto the stage, and everybody starts clapping. I guess they like our costumes, 'cuz who wouldn't? We stand side by side, and hold our cordless microphones in place, waiting for the track to begin. We smile at each other, and our eyes are screaming, "Omigod, look at all these people!"

Then the music comes on, and we start to sing:

"Some people walk with a panther
or strike a buffalo stance
that makes you wanna dance.

Other people flip the script
on the day of the jackal
that'll make you cackle . . ."

People start clapping to the beat. They like us! We even get our turns down, 'cuz Angie and I have been working real hard to improve our dance steps. I just wanna scream when Dorinda does her split—and gets right back up without splitting her pants. *Go, Dorinda!*

By the time we take our bows, to a huge round of applause, I feel almost like crying. *This* is why we love to sing—Angie and I have dreamed about moments like this all our lives!

"You were *fabulous*!" Ms. Dorothea screams when we get backstage. "I didn't hear one jackal cackle!"

"That's 'cuz he's in prison, eating his own tough hide right about now," Galleria humphs.

We all laugh at her joke. We know she's talking about Mr. Jackal Johnson—our brush with a real-live jackal. Mr. Johnson wanted to be our manager, but he didn't have good intentions. Lucky for us, Ms. Dorothea got wind of it before he had some Cheetah Girls for lunch. Like I told you, she doesn't play.

"I just *know* we're gonna win!" Chanel says, dancing around in the back while we wait for the rest of the performers to go on.

Pushing up the sleeves on their satin baseball jackets, those two annoying boys, Stak Chedda, posture like *they're* ready for Freddy, then walk out onstage like they think they're all that and a bag of fries.

"I know *you* ain't gonna win!" I say under

my breath, sucking my teeth behind their backs. We all start giggling, then huddle against the end of the curtain so we can hear them when the rap track drops.

"I *know* they got weak rhymes," Angie says, egging us on as they start to do their thing.

"Well, I'm the S to the T to the A to the K
Stak's my name and you know I got game.
When I'm on the mike, I make it sound so right
I rip the night till it gets way light
I think I'm gonna do it right now
So let's get to it—and if you wanna
Bust a rhyme, go ahead and do it!"

Even though the audience is doing a call and response with these cheesy rappers, we aren't worried about the competition, because their rap is, well, kinda like the alphabet—it starts with A, ends with Z, and gets real corny by the time they get to M.

Stak Chedda does get a lot of applause, but we're still not sweating it. "Get ready for Freddy, *girlitas*!" Galleria says. We do the Cheetah Girls handshake again, and wait for our cue to come out.

"Okay, ladies and gentlemen. It's that time again—time to pick the winner of this month's world-famous Apollo Amateur Hour contest. Come on out! Come on out!"

There's a drumroll, and we are all waved back onstage by the attendant. The lights are so bright, and there are so many people, it's kinda scary.

The announcer calls the name of each group in turn, and they step up to the center of the stage, so the audience can decide who should win the contest. Whoever gets the most applause wins.

"Lord, we need that prize money!" I say, grabbing Galleria's hand. "Just for once, I'd like to pay for my own tips."

Of course, I'm exaggerating, because we did spend some of the prize money we earned from the Cheetah-Rama show. But Daddy usually pays for us to get our hair and nails done twice a month. Maybe if we earned our own money, he wouldn't complain so much about having to pay the garage bill every month for two cars.

I'm getting so jittery I grab Angie's hand real tight. We both look at the front row, to see if we can spot Daddy. We were too nervous to look while we were performing.

Omigod, there he is! Angie and I give him a real big grin. Mr. Garibaldi is waving at us so hard, you'd think he was at the Santa Maria Parade in Houston.

I can't believe how many people are in this theater! I try not to look too far into the crowd, because the lights are so bright they almost blind me.

When the announcer calls our name to come up to the center of the stage, I really do think I'm gonna faint. We step forward, and I can see the little beads of sweat on the announcer's shiny forehead. He's wearing a red bow tie and a white shirt. His hair is slicked down, and his teeth are whiter than the neon sign outside.

I look around, trying to catch a glimpse of the Sandman. Where does he hide at, anyway?

"Okay, ladies and gentlemen. *You* decide. What did you think of the Cheetah Girls!" he bellows into the microphone.

The audience is clapping—louder than they did for Wesley Washington; Bacon, Once Over Lightly; or any of the other performers!

I'm so excited, I can't believe this is happening! We stand together at the back of the stage, and I can feel how excited all of us are by the sparkle in our eyes.

Now there is only one group left—and we know we got them beat by a bag of bacon bits!

"Okay, ladies and gentlemen—what did you think of the rapping duo, Stak Chedda!"

Of course, Popeye and his brother step forward like they own the place, but we know they ain't the cat's meow, as Big Momma would say.

All of a sudden I can't believe my ears. We look at one another in sudden shock when the audience claps louder for these bozos than they did for us!

The announcer's voice echoes like something right out of a horror movie—"And the winner of tonight's Amateur Hour contest at the world-famous *Apollo* Theatre is—STAK CHEDDA!"

"That's what I'm talking about!" Popeye yells into the mike, holding up his hands like he's Lavender Holy, the boxer, and he's just won a title bout.

I can feel the hot tears streaming down my face. *Why did tonight have to turn into Nightmare on 125th Street? Why?*

Chapter 5

Dorinda is crying, and she's not even trying to hide it. Bless her heart. She's probably kicking herself and thinking, Why didn't I take that job as a backup dancer for the Mo' Money Monique tour?

I can't blame her. For me and Angie, singing is our life. We *have* to sing—but Dorinda can *dance*. Maybe she doesn't even *want* to sing, but she's doing it for us, because *we* want her to.

Galleria looks so mad her mouth is poking out. I can't even look at Daddy right now. I feel so ashamed.

"Stak Chedda. They wuz more like Burnt Toast. This competition is rigged, yo!" Dorinda blurts out through her tears when we get backstage.

Ms. Dorothea doesn't say anything. She just holds Galleria, and then we all start crying.

"I can't believe we didn't win, Mommy," Galleria moans, tears streaming down her cheeks. She doesn't seem like herself at all—more like a little girl.

The attendant is now directing traffic, and sending everyone back up to the dressing rooms to get their belongings. "If you don't have anything in the dressing rooms, just move towards the rear exit. Do not try to exit in front!"

"Can we just stay here a minute?" Ms. Dorothea asks the attendant very nicely.

"Yes, go ahead, but you're gonna have to move shortly," she says briskly. She must have seen a million people like us, crying like babies just because they lost.

I don't know what we're gonna do now. We just can't seem to get a break! Angie and I wanted to sing gospel in the first place, but we got into pop and R&B music, because everybody kept telling us that was the only way to break into this business. Dag on, it seems like *rappers* are the only ones who are getting breaks now!

Mr. Garibaldi is waiting outside for us. "Your father went to get the car," he tells me and Angie, then turns to Galleria with his arms outstretched.

"Daddy! *Ci sono scemi.* I hate those people! Take me home!" Galleria is crying so hard, I can't believe it.

Angie is holding me now, because she is crying too. Chanel is holding Dorinda. People are standing around, looking at us. "Y'all were so cute!" this girl says to us as she walks out of the theater.

"Don't say nothing, Aisha. Can't you see they're crying? Leave them alone," her mother says, grabbing the girl's arm.

I look away from them. I don't care if we never come back here again!

Daddy pulls up outside the theater in the Bronco. Why couldn't he pull up down the block where no one could see us? Doesn't he understand how embarrassed we are? I don't want people looking at us, then laughing behind our backs.

I wish we hadn't worn our costumes here.

Then we could have changed back into our street clothes, and no one would have noticed us—the losers. "The Cheetah Girls."

I can't even look Daddy in the face when we get into the car. I try to sit in the back, but Chanel pushes me up front. She and Dorinda are *real* quiet now, slumped down in the back seat. They don't say a word.

"Those boys weren't that good. I don't see what all the fuss was about. You girls shoulda won," Daddy says, to no one in particular.

"Well, we didn't," I say, then sigh.

This is the worst day of my life. Worse than when Daddy first moved out of the house, and Ma stayed in bed crying for a week. Worse than when Grandma Winnie died from cancer. Worse than when I fell from the swing, and got seven stitches in my knee.

If you ask me, it doesn't really look like the Cheetah Girls are meant to be. I mean, we knew it would be hard, but not *this* hard. Every time we turn around, something is going wrong! "We can't get a break to save our lives," as Big Momma would say.

"Anybody want to go to Kickin' Chicken?" Daddy asks.

"No, thank you," we all say, one by one. I don't feel hungry at all. I just want to go home and get in bed, and pray to God to help us find some answers.

"You're cryin' all over your costume," Ms. Dorothea says to Galleria, reaching for a tissue out of her purse.

"I don't care about this stupid costume anymore!" Galleria blurts out between sobs.

We all get real quiet until Daddy stops in front of Dorinda's house at 116th Street. I feel bad that Dorinda has to live here, with all these people living on top of one another like cockroaches and always getting into each other's business.

Dorinda turns to ask Ms. Dorothea one more thing before she closes the car door. "How come they didn't like us?"

"They *did,*" Ms. Dorothea tells her. "But one day, they're gonna *love* you. You'll see. The world is cruel like that sometimes."

Ms. Dorothea gets out of the car, and gives Dorinda a big hug, and she doesn't let go for a long time. Ms. Dorothea looks like a big cheetah, and Dorinda looks like a little cub who is happy to be loved.

I hope Galleria doesn't feel jealous. She can be that way. Now she's acting like she doesn't even see them hug, and she doesn't even look up to say good-bye to Dorinda.

"Come here, *cara*," Mr. Garibaldi says to Galleria, then holds a tissue to Galleria's nose. She blows into it so hard it sounds like a fire engine siren.

Galleria is such a Daddy's girl—just like me and Angie—but her dad is a lot nicer than ours. I can't imagine Mr. Garibaldi getting as mean as Daddy gets sometimes. Now I feel more tears welling up—and these tears have nothing to do with the Cheetah Girls.

"Can I have one, Mr. Garibaldi?" I ask him, reaching for a tissue.

"Call me Franco," Mr. Garibaldi says, smiling at me with tears in his eyes as he hands me a tissue.

That is so sweet. He feels bad, just 'cuz his baby feels bad. He's always calling Galleria *cara*. I think that means *baby* in Italian. She's so lucky she gets to speak another language and all. That's one reason why she and Chanel seem so mysterious to us.

It gets real quiet again when it's just us and

Daddy in the car. He doesn't know how to say a lot of things to us. That's just how he is, 'cuz he has a lot of things on his mind—even though he does seem happier now that he has that girlfriend of his. He sure is crazy about her. Too bad we don't like her at all! Angie and I hold hands all the way home.

When we get home, Daddy lets us go right upstairs to bed, without saying anything. Good. I'm too tired now to even try to talk.

"I'm real proud of you girls," Daddy calls after us as we climb the stairs to our bedroom.

"Good night, Daddy," I say.

Daddy goes over to the stereo and puts on an LP. He loves this time of night. He likes to sit by himself, and smoke his pipe, and drink brandy while he watches television or listens to some music. He likes to listen to the legends like Miles Davis, Lionel Hampton, and Coltrane late at night, 'cuz, he says, that's when you can really hear "the jazz men trying to touch you with their music."

"Good night, Daddy," Angie says, and we continue on upstairs.

Angie is real quiet as we change into our pajamas. She doesn't even make any jokes about the shoe boxes in the closet. I wish Mr. Teddy Poodly could come out of his shoe box and dance with us right now. Anything would be better than this misery.

I go to my shoe box and look at it, then decide to take the Scotch tape off it. If Mr. Teddy Poodly wants to come out and dance, let him—he just better not bother Porgy and Bess, our pet guinea pigs.

After I throw the Scotch tape in the wastebasket, Angie and I kneel down by our beds. Tonight, it's Angie's turn to lead our prayer.

"God, please help us see why you didn't let us win the contest tonight," she says. "If you don't want us to be singers anymore, please let us know. Just show us the signs. We'll do real good in school so that we can go to college, like we said. If you don't want us to quit singing, then please give us strength to do better, so we can stay in New York and not let Ma down.

"Please look over her in Houston, and Big Momma, and Granddaddy Walker, too, because his blood pressure is acting up, and he didn't sound too good on the phone. Oh, and please tell us if High Priestess Abala Shaballa is a witch—and if she is, if she is a *good* witch. Just give us the signs. We'll understand. Amen."

After we say our prayers, Angie and I curl up in our beds. We reach out to each other, and hold hands across the space between—just like we did when we were little, and would get afraid of a lightning storm.

"I wish Ma was here," I whisper to Angie.

"Me, too."

"I wish Grandma Winnie was here," I add, crying.

"Me, too."

And that's the last thing either of us says before going to sleep.

The next morning, when I wake up, I feel bad already. That's when I realize that what happened last night wasn't just a bad dream—it was a waking nightmare! If somebody came to me right now with an Aladdin's lamp or something like that, I would wish that last night never happened, even if it meant that Freddy would have to visit me in my dreams.

How could God let all our dreams get shattered just like that?

On Sunday mornings we are usually so happy to get up, because we go to church and we go to Hallelujah Tabernacle, and they let me and Angie do two-part harmony songs on "teen Sundays." Also, during convocation season, we get to sing in the choir sometimes.

Right now, my hair looks a mess. I was so upset last night, I forgot to put the stocking cap on my head to keep my wrap smooth. I hate when I do that!

"Angie, those are my shoes!" I yell, as she tries to sneak her feet into my black pumps instead of hers. She can be such a copycat sometimes—trying to act like she doesn't know her things from mine. She's always trying to switch stuff—especially when she loses a button, or scuffs her shoes bad.

I know Angie is real upset, because she doesn't even pretend like she *didn't* know she was putting on my shoes. She just sits on the edge of the bed and waits for me to put on my clothes.

I reach for the navy blue dress with the gold buckle, because that's what we decided we would wear. When we go to church, we *always* dress alike, and we can't wear pants. "Do you think Daddy is gonna let us be Cheetah Girls anymore?" Angie asks, real quiet.

"I don't know, Angie, but I bet you he's gonna call Ma and tell her we lost." I open the bottom drawer of the white chest of drawers to get out a pair of navy blue panty hose. I feel so bad, my head hurts when I talk. I hold up the panty hose and run my fingers through them.

"Dag on, Angie, these have a run in them!" Sucking my teeth, I throw the panty hose in the white wicker wastebasket under the night-stand. "It's a good thing I checked before I wasted my time putting them on. I told you not to put tights *back* in the drawer if you put a run in them!"

"I musta not noticed!" Angie exclaims, getting real defensive. Then I give her that look we have between us, and Angie cracks a little smile. She knows I know when she's lying. I don't know why she even bothers sometimes.

"Don't forget," I mutter. "It's your turn to clean Porgy and Bess's cage."

I can smell the bacon frying downstairs. High Priestess Abala came over this morning, and she's cooking breakfast for us. She's going to *church* with us, too, believe it or not! I think that's pretty strange, considering all her weird rituals and stuff. To tell you the truth, I wish she wasn't here, because I don't feel like being nice to anybody this morning.

"What if we had been on that stage by ourselves, Angie?" I ask, as walk out the bedroom door to go downstairs and eat breakfast. "We woulda frozen solid like a pair of icicles!"

Angie just nods at me. I know that means we're both thinking the same thing—what will we do if we aren't the Cheetah Girls anymore?

The spiral staircase in our duplex is *real* steep, so we always come downstairs slow and careful. (I'm afraid of heights. So is Angie.)

"Omigod!" Angie gasps when we get to the bottom landing. "I *know* the Evil One is in our house now."

"What's the matter, Angie?" I ask, trying not to bump into her from behind.

"What *is* that thing?" Angie asks.

I take a few steps forward, so I can see what it is she's talking about. Then I let out a loud, surprised scream. This ugly thing—some kind of huge, horrible mask—is hanging on the wall in front of us. It gave me such a fright it almost scared me to death—right into Granddaddy Walker's funeral parlor back home!

"Good morning, ladies," High Priestess Abala Shaballa says, walking from the kitchen into the living room. Angie and I get our manners back *real* fast, because we know that Abala musta had something to do with this strange thing hanging on the wall. It's just as weird as she is.

"Good morning, Abala," I say politely, making myself be nice to her, even though I don't want to. I hope Daddy didn't tell her that we lost the Apollo Amateur Hour contest. How *could* we lose that? I *still* can't believe those boys won! "The devil is a liar," just like Big Momma says.

"Do you know what this is?" High Priestess Abala Shaballa asks, pointing to the thing on the wall.

"No, I—we—don't," I say, looking at Angie for some support. Now that Abala is Daddy's girlfriend, it just seems like we never know anything anymore.

It's not like before. At least, in the old days, Daddy, Angie and I got to learn things together. Now it seems like everything new he knows, he learned from her.

"It's a Bogo Mogo Hexagone Warrior Mask," Abala says proudly.

No wonder it's strange, I think. It's something named after *her*.

"You see the markings here," Abala continues, pointing to the bright red marks across the cheeks of the big mask, which looks like the head of a space alien.

"Yes, I see them," I respond, trying to act interested, even though I know there is something deep-down weird about this thing.

"When the markings change colors, it means it's time for Hexagone to reign once again, and the world will become a magical place. With Bogo Mogo here, you will have someone to watch over you all the time now."

Oh, *great*. Now we not only have Daddy, we have this thing's beady eyes watching us, too. I try not to look scared.

"You *do* believe in magic, don't you, Aquanette?"

"Yes, High Priestess Abala," I say. I don't tell her what I really think—that she needs some more magic lessons, because Mr. Teddy Poodly didn't come out of his shoe box to help us win the contest. So why should this mask do anything—except maybe scare me in the middle of the night when I come downstairs to get a snack?

"Well, let's go eat. I've fixed a divine feast for the two of you," High Priestess Abala says, outstretching her arms the way she does, like a peach tree with big ol' branches. (Grandma Winnie had one in her backyard, with the biggest, juicy peaches we ever ate . . . then it just withered up and died when grandma did.)

"Good morning, Daddy," I say as we join him in the kitchen. I'm still not able to look him in the eye. I wonder if he told High Priestess Abala that we lost the contest. Dag on, how *could* we?

Angie and I sit down at the dining room table real quiet, and High Priestess Abala serves us some ham, eggs, biscuits, and fried apples. Then, for herself and Daddy, she pours some green stuff from the blender into two glasses.

I can't believe that's all Daddy is eating for breakfast! He used to eat a whole plate of bacon and tin of biscuits, with a whole pot of coffee! Daddy looks into Abala's eyes all goo-goo-eyed, and they clink their glasses of green goo together. Yuck!

"To you, my divine Priestess—because I've never felt younger," Daddy says, then gulps down his shake.

I just hope he doesn't start looking younger, or I'm gonna call Granddaddy Walker to come up here and make sure Abala's not slipping embalming fluid in Daddy's blender! (Granddaddy Walker says that's why dead people look so good—sometimes even better than they did in real life!)

Thank God, the phone rings before these two lovebirds fly over the cuckoo's nest together. Daddy answers, then hands the phone to me. "It's your friend," he says.

"Hello?" I say, taking the receiver.

"Aqua, you're not gonna believe this," Galleria says, without even saying hello. I can't believe how much better she sounds!

"What?" I reply.

"Mom just had her hair done at Churl, It's You! and Pepto B., her hairdresser, told her that *he's* hooking up Kahlua Alexander's braids later!"

"Really?" I answer, but I still don't understand why Galleria is so excited.

"So guess who he's gonna hook *us* up with?"

"No! *Kahlua?"* I gasp. You *know* I'm surprised, but now I'm getting excited, too.

"That's right, dee-light. We have hatched a plan. Mom says for you and Angie to be ready by six o'clock, 'cuz 'Operation Kahlua' is in full effect."

"Okay," I respond, even though I'm still not sure what she's talking about.

"And Aqua—don't wear the same clothes you and Angie wear to church, okay?"

"I know that, Galleria."

"Wear the cheetah jumpers and the ballet flats, okay?"

"Okay, Galleria. Bye!"

When I hang up the phone, I'm smiling from ear to ear. Angie, of course, knows something is up.

"Galleria is picking us up at six o'clock," I say, smiling at Daddy. "We should thank God we have Galleria, because I've never seen anyone rise from the dead faster than her!"

Now Abala is looking at me like she approves, but I don't want to give her the wrong idea. "That's just an expression Granddaddy Walker uses," I explain. "She didn't *really* rise from the dead."

"Your granddaddy is wise, because there are more ways than one to levitate your fate," Abala says, sipping on her witches' brew. "There is nothing for you to worry about, my dears. Bogo Mogo magic is working for you. If not today, then surely tomorrow."

Well, I sure hope Mr. Bogo Mogo can do his wonders from the bottom of a garbage can, 'cuz that's where he's ending up.

Chapter 6

It's so nice of Galleria's folks to offer to pick us up and take us to Pepto B.'s salon, Churl, It's You! Otherwise, Daddy would have probably insisted that *he* drive us. He thinks seven o'clock is kinda late for us to be out without a chaperone! Dag on, even Chanel can come home unescorted up until nine o'clock on school nights, and her mother is kinda strict. Our Daddy takes the cobbler, though.

I shoulda known something was up, though, when Galleria rings the bell at six o'clock. We're not due at the salon till seven thirty, and it only takes ten minutes to get there.

"Toodles to the poodles! You *fab-yoo-luss*

Walker twins, *we've* got a surprise for you!" Galleria says in her funny Southern accent.

She is definitely feeling better because she's acting like herself. And when Galleria acts like herself, the whole world is a brighter place. Even the cheetahs in the jungle are probably smiling right now.

Angie and I have been feeling better too, because Reverend Butter's sermon at church today did us a world of good. We crowd the front doorway of our building, waiting for Ms. Dorothea, Chanel, and Mr. Garibaldi to come in.

"You're so lucky you don't live in an elevator building," Dorinda comments, coming in and kissing us hello.

That's the truth. I would be scared to have to go up in an elevator every time I wanna get to my apartment. Like I told you, Angie and I are afraid of heights. That's why Daddy got a ground floor apartment in a townhouse.

It's quiet on our block, and we got a nice view of Riverside Park, so at least it feels a little like back home. I don't know if I could take all that noise over where Dorinda lives.

It's good to hear a pigeon chirping every now and again.

Ms. Dorothea is taking some garment bags and stuff from the van, and Chanel is helping her carry them inside. Chanel works part time at Toto in New York . . . Fun in Diva Sizes, 'cuz she has to pay her mother back all the money she charged on her credit card.

See, I think Chanel lost her mind after we did that first show at the Cheetah-Rama. She started shoppin' till we wuz *all* droppin'! I guess Chanel thought everything was gonna come real easy. But it's not—you gotta work *real* hard just to hold onto your dream. By the time she came to her senses, Chanel owed her mother a whole lot of money! Lucky for her, Ms. Dorothea offered her the job at her store.

"What's that?" Angie asks, pointing to the garment bags.

"You didn't think we were gonna let you wear just plain ol' anything to meet the biggest singer in the world, did you?" Galleria asks, batting her eyelashes.

"Now, I was gonna surprise you girls with your new outfits after you won the Apollo Amateur contest. But that was their loss. And anyway, now we have bigger prey to pounce on," Ms. Dorothea says, all optimistic and funny like she is. Opening the garment bag, she pulls out matching fake fur cheetah miniskirts and vests.

"Oooh!" Angie exclaims, putting her hands on her cheeks, like she does after she opens her Christmas presents.

"We're gonna go in there looking like a *real* group," says Galleria, all proud. Then she pulls a tube of lipstick out of her cheetah backpack. "Look at the new shade of S.N.A.P.S. lipstick we got. It's called 'Video.'"

"Oooh—it's got silver sparkles!" I say, grabbing the tube. I never saw silver lipstick like this before. "So what are we gonna do at the hair salon—act like we're getting our hair done?" Knowing Galleria and Ms. Dorothea, there has to be some plan.

Galleria, Chanel, and Dorinda look at each other like I just ate a whole peach cobbler pie without offering them a slice.

"No, silly, we're gonna go in there and *sing* while Kahlua's getting her hair done," Galleria pipes up.

"Ohhhhh," Angie and I say in unison.

"That's right. That's a good plan. Then what?"

"Then Miss Kahlua Alexander will be so inclined to wave her magic wand—and have her fairy godmother help us . . . I don't know, get a record deal . . . or at least a 'Happy Meal!'"Galleria says, waving her hand like it's a wand.

"We know that's right," I chuckle. Kahlua Alexander is the *biggest* singer, and she can do just about anything with all her "magic powers."

"Operation Kahlua will be in full effect," Galleria says, smiling. Then she whispers to me, "Ask your Dad if it's okay for us to practice here."

"Right here?" I ask, smiling. That's Galleria—when she has a plan, there is no telling *what* she'll do to make it happen!

"Come on. We can sing two songs—'Wannabe Stars,' because we know it so well, and the new song, 'More Pounce to the Ounce.'"

I hesitate a little, because I don't know if we're ready to sing Galleria's new song yet.

"Come on, Angie. We're ready. We've been practicing it for two long weeks!" Galleria begs me, reading my thoughts.

"*I'll* ask Daddy!" Angie says all excited, running toward the den, where Daddy is sitting with High Priestess Abala Shaballa.

Dag on, she's over here a lot now. Doesn't she have some new spells to practice at home?

Daddy and his High Priestess come into the living room with Angie tagging behind them. "Greetings, sacred ones," Abala greets our guests.

She gives Ms. Dorothea a little bow. Those two met at Dorinda's adoption party, and I don't think Ms. Dorothea likes the High Priestess too much. High Priestess is even taller than Ms. Dorothea, if you can believe that—even with Dorothea's new hairdo, which is higher than a skyscraper! Abala is so tall she looks like a weeping willow tree, ready to sway if the wind blows in her direction!

Abala turns to Galleria, Dorinda, and Chanel. "Tell me, sacred ones," she says. "Did the Vampire Spell work?"

Abala does look real pretty today—kinda like a . . . well, a High Priestess I guess. She does have real pretty eyes too. I guess I can see why Daddy likes her so much.

"No," I volunteer sourly. Daddy *musta* told

her by now that we lost the contest. Why is she asking us if the spell worked?

"Then either you didn't follow my directions, or High Priestess Hexagone has bigger plans for you," High Priestess Abala Shaballa says solemnly.

Galleria mumbles under her breath, "Whatever makes you clever."

Finally, Daddy senses the situation is a little tense, because he pipes up, "Listen, girls, I know you have to get ready. My home is yours, and do whatever you need to do to get ready. We'll be in the kitchen if you need anything. Come on, Abala," he says, touching her arm gently.

That makes me feel real proud. Daddy still believes in us! He never says much, but I guess that's just his way.

"Aah, che bella!" Mr. Garibaldi says, looking at Daddy's snow globe collection. "May I touch?"

"Go ahead," I say with a smile, looking at Galleria, who is rolling her eyes to the ceiling. I think her Daddy still loves the snow.

"Just don't start collecting them, Daddy," Galleria giggles.

* * *

After we practice for one hour, we climb into the van. I guess, you could say, we are ready for Freddy—and definitely for Kahlua Alexander!

"I can't *believe* how high Pepto teased my wig this time!" Ms. Dorothea says, looking in the mirror on the dashboard. "It looks like a torpedo ready for takeoff!"

We just chuckle and look at each other. I mean, Ms. Dorothea's hair does look a little like a skyscraper, but if anyone has the personality to carry it off, she does.

"Honey, he is so lucky I didn't pull a diva fit! But then he let the glass slipper drop—that Miss Kahlua is in town, to make a movie called *Platinum Pussycats*, with Bertha Kitten. He *also* let it slip that he is giving Kahlua a new 'do, because Bertha, or 'Miss Kitten' to you, said 'those braids have to go.' So I just started pouncing instead of pouting."

"But how did you angle an intro?" Dorinda asks.

Angie and I look at each other, like, "there they go again, saying things we don't understand!"

"Pepto was complaining about how his

mother just couldn't find the right dress for her thirtieth wedding anniversary," Ms. Dorothea explains. "So, naturally, I volunteered to make the dress of Ms. Butworthy's dreams—*for free!* Darling, Pepto and I have played this cat-and-mouse game for *years*, and believe me, his mother is no Happy Meal. She's such a pain, she's probably banned from every diva-size department in the country."

"Ohhhh, so that's what the "B" stands for," Dorinda says, smiling.

"Mr. B. speaks way too fast to get his whole last name out!" Ms. Dorothea says smiling. "You'll see."

As we pull up in front of the Churl, It's You! hair salon on 57th Street, Ms. Dorothea takes a deep breath, and announces, "Okay, girls, it's time to give them more 'pounce for the ounce!'"

"Ooh, look at how *la dopa* this place is!" Chanel exclaims as we approach Churl, It's You! "I'm gonna bring Princess Pamela here!"

The pink lights in the Churl, It's You! sign are so bright they sparkle like stars. In the window, there are floating brown mannequin heads with pink, blue, yellow, green, and purple wigs!

"Ooh, Angie—look at the heads!" I say, ogling the window display. "Look at the beautiful sign! We don't have anything like this in Houston."

"A blue Afro?" Angie says, smiling. Blue is our favorite color, but neither of us would have the nerve to wear a wig like that on our head. Galleria and Chanel would, of course. I wish we were more like them. They have so much style—but I have to admit, we *all* look fierce in our matching Cheetah Girl outfits.

Of course, Chanel runs to the door first, and we have to hurry to catch up to her. "Wait up, yo!" Dorinda snaps.

"Chuchie, we have to make an entrance *together*," Galleria says, taking the lead.

When Galleria opens the big glass door, musical chimes go off, and a recording starts playing: "Churl, It's You! Work the blue! Think pink like I do! Get sheen with green! We love—guess who!"

"Ooh, that is so dope!" laughs Dorinda.

"*Ay, Dios mío*, the whole place is pink. *Qué bonita!*" exclaims Chanel, looking around the salon like she's in a candy store. Pink is one of her favorite colors, and her whole bedroom is pink. She even has a pink cheetah bedspread!

"Wait till Kahlua sees your braids," I say to Chanel proudly, because she *looks* like Kahlua, with her braids and pretty eyes and all—she's just a lighter complexion.

"Welcome to Churl, It's You!" says a nice lady wearing a pink dress with an apron over it. Even her *shoes* are pink—and so is her *hair*!

"Hi, darling," Ms. Dorothea says, extending her hand to the pink lady. "We have an appointment with Pepto B."

"Yes, of course. So nice to see you again, Mrs. Garibaldi. Right this way. You must be the Cheetah Girls," she says, looking at us.

"Yes, ma'am," Angie says, giving the lady a big smile.

We look around the salon in wonder as we walk to the back. There are two huge cases with pink cotton candy, pink soda, and bags of pink popcorn! The hair dryer helmets are pink, and so are the chairs—even the sink where you get your hair washed!

"Oooh, look at the pink jukebox," I exclaim. The salon we go to doesn't have a jukebox. It's *boring* compared to this. "We have to ask Daddy to let us come here and get our hair done!" I whisper to Angie.

"It's even doper than Princess Pamela's!" Angie whispers back. "But don't tell Chanel I said so."

"I can't believe we're gonna meet Kahlua!" I say. We grab each other's hand and give a quick, tight squeeze, and I know Angie's thinking the same thing.

All of a sudden, a brown-skinned man with a short, pink Afro comes running over to us. He kisses Ms. Dorothea on both cheeks. I've never seen anyone do that before, except in the movies. He must be French or something. Then he turns real quick, and says to us, "Pepto B., that's me!"

We are just tickled—well, pink, I guess! As we introduce ourselves to Pepto B., I suddenly don't feel so nervous anymore.

Pepto B. grabs Ms. Dorothea's arm and whispers loudly, "Churl, your timing is *purrfect*. I just finished putting in Kahlua's weave. Wait till you see it. Churl, it took two hours to get those braids outta her hair! You woulda thought they were stuck on with Krazy

Glue! But you know those *Hollywood* hairdressers—you need a magician to fix your hair after they get through with you!"

Pepto B. and Ms. Dorothea dissolve into fits of giggles. Angie and I are just staring at them.

"Close your mouth, Aqua and Angie!" hisses Galleria. She says we watch people with our mouths open sometimes. I guess we do, but she has to understand—we're not used to all the ways of the Big Apple, the way she and Chanel are!

After the two grown-ups finish "cutting up," as Big Momma calls it, Pepto B. puts his hand on his chest and says, "Churl, you're killing me. Can you believe Bertha Kitten is coming out of her hermetically sealed coffin to do a movie? *Churrrl*, believe it!"

Then he turns to us, and says the words we've been waiting to hear—"And now, if you all are ready, it's time to meet the one and only . . . Kahlua!"

Chapter 7

When we get to the back of the salon, Kahlua is seated in the beauty parlor chair, reading a magazine. Standing next to her by the counter is a lady in a light-blue sweatsuit. That must be her mother, I figure. I heard she's managing Kahlua now, and that they even started a production company called "Kahlua's Korporation."

All of a sudden, I feel *real* nervous again. My stomach starts getting queasy, while my brain is screaming: *"It's really her!* "

Kahlua looks up at us, all curious, and says, "Hi!"

Oooo, she's even prettier in person than in her music videos! Staring at Kahlua, I wonder how she keeps her skin so smooth like that. It's the prettiest chocolate shade I've ever seen. She must be about a shade lighter than me and Angie. No, maybe two shades lighter, because she's got a lotta makeup on.

"Close your mouth, Angie!" Galleria whispers behind me, and pokes me in the butt.

Then Kahlua's mother introduces herself to Ms. Dorothea. "Hi, I'm Aretha Alexander. And who are all these cute girls?" she asks, smiling like a curious cat.

"We're the Cheetah Girls!" Galleria bursts out, giggling.

"Do you sing?" Kahlua asks, smiling now from ear to ear.

"Yes, churl, they do," Pepto B. offers, butting in. "And you should let them sing while I finish. I could sure use some entertainment, after fixing this tragedy that was up in yo' hair!"

We all giggle—even Kahlua—and she has the cutest dimples when she smiles, just like Dorinda's.

"Pepto, you are so *wrong*—but you are *right*," Kahlua says, all bubbly. "After putting up with *you* for four hours, I could use some entertainment!"

"Oh, don't let me take this comb and use it like a forklift on your head, churl!" Pepto B. warns, putting his hands on his hips.

After we all finish giggling, Ms. Dorothea clears her throat and says, "I guess it's time for growl power, girls!"

"'Growl Power!' Oooo, that is so cute!" Kahlua exclaims.

Ms. Dorothea takes our cheetah backpacks and puts them in the corner. Then the five of us huddle together, right there in the middle of the beauty salon, and sing *a capella* (that means without our instrumental track) the song we have practiced fifty million times, "Wanna-be Stars in the Jiggy Jungle."

I wish Ma could see us now—singing in the beauty parlor again, just like we used to when we were three years old, sitting in the double stroller next to her while she got her hair done.

Everybody claps when we're done—even the customers under the hair dryers!

"You wrote that song yourselves?" Kahlua's mother asks, and you can tell she is real impressed.

"*She* did," I say excitedly, pointing to Galleria.

Galleria looks like she's blushing, and I can tell Chanel feels a little bit jealous. Those two fight like sisters—more than Angie and I do—and we *are* sisters!

I think Chanel wants to be the leader of our group, and that's why she's jealous. I guess she's gonna have to learn how to write songs, instead of charging up clothes on her mother's credit card!

"Do y'all have another song?" Kahlua asks excitedly.

"Churl, I hear they got more songs than my jukebox!" Pepto B. says as he teases Kahlua's hair.

Ms. Dorothea looks at us, and motions for us to sing again. "We haven't performed this song before," Galleria says, then looks at us. "I, um, just finished writing it a few weeks ago."

"Go, ahead, we love it!" Ms. Alexander says, egging us on.

On the count of three, we then sing "More Pounce to the Ounce." I can feel my hands sweating, because singing a capella is a lot harder than singing with tracks—especially when you have five-part harmonies. See, you have to make sure everybody sings on the same level, and my and Angie's voices tend to be a little stronger than theirs are.

"Snakes in the grass have no class
but Cheetah Girls have all the swirls.
To all the competition, what can we say?
You had your day, so you'd better bounce, y'all,
While you still got some flounce, y'all,
'Cuz Cheetah Girls got more pounce to the ounce y'all!!"

After we finish the song, I look over at Angie. She leaned a little too hard on the chorus, I think—but I'll tell her that later. I think we still sounded good, though, because Kahlua and her mother are grinning from ear to ear.

"I love y'all!" Kahlua exclaims. "You got a record deal?"

We shake our heads "no."

I just wanna scream, *Get us a deal, please!*

"Momma, let's talk to Mr. Hitz about them," Kahlua says to her mother. Mrs. Alexander nods her head in agreement. "He's the president of the label I'm on—Def Duck Records," Kahlua explains.

"That would be groovy like a movie!" Galleria says, jumping up and down, she's so excited. Then she kisses Kahlua on the cheek, and gives her a big hug.

"You have so much energy—doesn't she, Momma?" Kahlua asks, her slanty eyes getting wide. "She reminds me of Backstabba a little, don't you think so?"

People have always thought Galleria looks a lot like Backstabba, the lead singer of Karma's Children. That band comes from our hometown—and Angie and I have decided we're not going back until we become as big as them!

"How did y'all become the Cheetah Girls?" Kahlua asks.

We tell Kahlua all about the jiggy jungle, growl power, and our Cheetah Girls rules and council meetings. She just loves it—especially when Galleria tells her about the dream she's had since she's a little girl:

"We wanna go to Africa and start a Cheetah conservancy. When we get rich, we're gonna get lots and lots of acres of land, so all the cheetahs in the jungle can live there and just chill, without worrying about anything. Then we'll travel all over the world, singing to peeps on two legs *and* four!"

"You are *too much,*" Kahlua says, crossing her legs and waving her hand at Galleria. Kahlua has nice nails. I bet you they're tips, though—like mine.

I'm looking at the chip on my nail when I hear Galleria blurt out, "We performed at the Apollo Amateur Hour Contest Saturday night—and we lost!"

How could she say something so dumb? I wonder. Why is she telling Kahlua that?

But Kahlua's reaction is the last thing I expected. "Honey, that's nothing. *I* lost it, too!" she says. "You know, the record company doesn't let me talk about it in interviews, but Momma will tell you—I cried like a baby for two weeks after I lost!"

Kahlua is beside herself laughing now. "You know how many famous recording artists have performed at the Apollo Amateur Hour Contest and lost?"

"How many?" Dorinda asks, her eyes wide with wonder.

"Let's see—Toyz II Boyz, The Moonpies, even Karma's Children lost!" Kahlua says, nodding her head like she knows things we don't.

"*What!?* " I say, all surprised. "I didn't know that!"

"No—no one is gonna tell you about their failures, but you have to stick to your dreams in this business, girls—'cuz people will trample on them like elephants!"

Kahlua sips her soda, then looks at Galleria's lips real close. "What color lipstick is that you're wearing?"

"Video. It's dope, right?" Galleria says, beaming.

"Oooo, I haven't seen this one yet! Can I try it?"

"Wait, I'll get it." Galleria runs to get her cheetah backpack, to show Kahlua the new shade of S.N.A.P.S. lipstick we're all wearing.

"Y'all look so cute in those outfits," Kahlua says, putting on the lipstick. Then she and Galleria start "ooooing" and "aaahing" up a storm.

"Tell us about your cheetah-licious movie," Galleria says, egging Kahlua on, now that they're like two peas in a pod.

"It's *such* hard work, you can't believe it! I

have to get up at five o'clock in the morning tomorrow to start shooting," Kahlua says. Then she starts playacting a yawn, and leans on Pepto B.'s shoulders for a hug.

"How are they going to get that 'Mummy' Bertha Kitten to the set on time?" Pepto B. quips. "Churl, she better be *grateful* she got this gig, 'cuz the only thing *she's* been doing for the last thirty years is her nails! She gives you any trouble, we'll sic these Cheetah Girls on her!"

We all hug each other good-bye, then do the Cheetah Girls handshake with Kahlua, Pepto B., and Mrs. Alexander—which they all just *love*. Ms. Dorothea gives Mrs. Alexander her business card, and they hug good-bye.

"We'll let you know what happens," Mrs. Alexander says, "but you don't have to worry, Dorothea. Your Cheetah Girls have 'more pounce for the ounce,' just like they said. The other girl groups won't stand a chance, once the Cheetahs show up."

Mr. Garibaldi is waiting for us outside in his van. "How did it go? *Bene?*" he asks Galleria as we get in the car. But he already knows the answer, from our big grins. "I knew it. That's why I made you girls a fresh batch of chocolate cannolis—Aqua's favorite," he says, handing us a big box of Italian pastries.

We all look at Galleria and burst out laughing. I munch on my dee-licious treats, which I shouldn't be eating, because Daddy doesn't like us to eat anything two hours before we practice—and I *know* we have to practice tonight before we go to bed. He let us off the hook last night—but lightning doesn't strike twice in the same place!

I give Angie a look, and she knows what I'm trying to say—*Don't tell Daddy we ate these!* The one thing I love about Angie is, she sure can keep a secret.

"Darlings, isn't this place something?" Ms. Dorothea says to me and Angie. She points to a beautiful skyscraper with a tiny, brightly lit tower topped by a steeple.

"It sure is," I respond, ogling the tower like it's a secret place in a castle or something. "You know, Ms. Dorothea, I thought for sure it was all over for us when we lost that contest."

"I know," Ms. Dorothea says with a sigh. "You take one wrong turn on the road to your dreams, and all of a sudden, you're in hyena territory. Then you stumble upon a right turn, and there it is right before your eyes—"

"—that magical, cheetah-licious place called the jiggy jungle," Galleria pipes in. Then, chuckling, she adds, "Your one-way ticket to *get-paid paradise*!"

Chapter 8

Biology class is my favorite class at school, besides vocal, but I have no interest today in cutting open a frog—and that's not like me at all. I know we shouldn't expect anything to come from our meeting with Kahlua, but dag on! We can't think about anything else!

We pray to God every night to please give us one itty-bitty sign—anything—even a shoe falling from the sky and hitting us over the head would be good enough!

It seems like *years* since "Operation Kahlua," and now we're down in the bottom of the crab barrel again, just moping around, trying not to get bit by the other crabs.

Look at this poor little frog, I think. He is just

lying there dead, on his back, waiting to be cut open. "I wonder if you can tell if someone tried to choke it and murder it or something. You know—'frog autopsy,'" I chuckle to Paula Pitts. She's my biology classmate, and we record all our experiments together.

"The eyeballs *are* kinda big—it does look like something scared it a little before it—you know—croaked," Paula says, all sad. "I don't know what you find so interesting about looking inside of bodies, Aqua. I think it's creepy."

Paula is a drama major, and she wants to be an actress, so she can be a little dramatic at times. "I hardly call opening a frog cadaver *The Night of the Living Dead*," I quip back. "Miss Paula, you are acting like the Pitts again."

I always tease her. She gets so squeamish, and she just doesn't like biology class or science projects the way I do. She likes to slink around, "like she's the cat's meow on Catfish Row," as Big Momma would say. Opening her big brown eyes wide, Paula asks, "You heard anything from Kahlua yet?"

She just loves to talk about show business. *Everybody* at school knows about our meeting with Kahlua—including JuJu Beans Gonzalez, who really cuts her eyes at us now.

I can't blame her for being so jealous of us. Angie and I are kinda popular at LaGuardia, I guess, because we're twins and come from Houston—even though there are kids at our school from all over the country.

The kids here nicknamed us SWV—Sisters With Voices—because, I guess, we do sing up a storm, if I say so myself. We're getting real good training here at LaGuardia, too—singing pop and classical music, which is good for our range. When we were younger, we kinda had our hearts set on singing gospel, but like I said, it just seems like pop and R&B music get more attention in the business.

That's why we got together with the Cheetah Girls. We thought about it real hard, and talked to Ma, and Big Momma, and everybody else about it before we made up our minds. Now we just don't know if we made the right decision.

Letting out a big sigh, I turn to Paula and moan, "This whole thing is like a big roller coaster ride. When you're on top, it's the greatest feeling in the world. But when you get ready to roll to the bottom, you'd better strap yourself in and start screaming your head off again, because it feels so *scary*."

"Yeah, you gotta kiss a lot of frogs in show business before you get anywhere," Paula agrees with a sigh. "That's how I feel in drama class sometimes, too. I give until it hurts, and it never feels like enough." Now she's fiddling around with the knob on the microscope, and her face is pained, like she's getting ready for her monologue. She is so *dramatic*.

"Ooh, look at his little lungs," I exclaim, finally getting excited by Freddy the frog's insides.

Then I feel a wave of pity come over me. "Freddy, I hope your little dreams came true before you left this earth," I mutter. "I hope all of our dreams come true. . . ."

After school, Angie always waits for me outside, and I can tell by her long face that she's still feeling down at the bottom of the crab barrel. "I wish we could go to Pappadeux's and get some Cajun crawfish right about now," I moan.

She nods her head like she could put a bib on

and chow down, too. They've got everything in New York except Pappadeux's—and *I'm sorry*, but nobody makes crawfish like they do. You get a big ol' pot of Cajun crawfish, with pieces of corn on the cob, and small red potatoes, and all this spicy juice. Then you just crack the itty-bitty shells in your hands, and suck out those tasty "chil'rens," as Big Momma calls them. Those were some of the best times we ever had as a family, going there on Friday nights for dinner. Everybody would come—Uncle Skeeter, Big Momma, Grandma Winnie, Ma, and all our cousins, too.

"I don't understand why we have to go to Drinka Champagne's Conservatory today," Angie says sheepishly. "What's the use of practicing if we're not performing anywhere?

"I know that's right, but you know what Galleria says. We should be practicing more, just in case we get to perform somewhere, for somebody, *somehow*."

My voice trails off, because I see the newspaper in Angie's hand, and I realize we haven't read our horoscope today.

"What's it say?" I ask, as we cross the street to catch the subway.

I hope it's not real crowded today, I think, as we wait to ride the IRT down to Drinka's. Dag on, there are so many people on the sidewalks and subway platforms in New York, you feel like you're gonna get trampled or something!

"Dag on, don't you know what page it's on by now?" I say, getting annoyed at Angie, who is still fumbling with the newspaper as we get on the crowded train. But why I'm really upset is because this man with a big ol' briefcase keeps knocking into me like I'm a rag doll.

"Here it is," Angie says, all serious, like she's getting ready to give a sermon in church. Sometimes she is so *slow*! "Let's see. 'Get ready for a big unexpected trip. You're gonna be flying the friendly skies real soon. Pack your party clothes!'"

"Oh, great, that just means we gotta go home to Houston for Thanksgiving, and do something *real* exciting, like work in Big Momma's garden. We know that," I say, curling my upper lip. (Angie and I both do that sometimes when we get mad.)

Angie gets quiet and closes the newspaper. She doesn't have to tell me. I know she feels disappointed, too.

We normally don't go to Drinka Champagne's Conservatory on school nights. But they have a new choreographer, and she can only work with us tonight, because she's working on Sista Fudge's new music video all weekend. Sista Fudge is one of our favorite singers, because she can "scream and testify"—back home, that's what we say when a singer can really *wail*, and has vocal "chops."

But we're not here studying singing. We're here to get our *moves* down. See, Galleria is always fussing at us to get the dance steps right. It's very important when you put on a show to have real good choreography—to give people something to watch. That's just as important when you perform as how you sing.

Since Angie and I are the background singers, we don't have to dance as much as Dorinda, Chanel, and Galleria, but we all have to do the same dance steps.

"Hi, Miss Winnie," I say, smiling to the receptionist at Drinka's as we enter the building. I like Miss Winnie, because she's real nice, and she has the same name as our grandma who passed.

The rest of the Cheetah Girls have already

changed into their leotards, and are waiting in Studio A for us. They are huddled together in one corner, while the rest of the class is on the other side.

After we do our Cheetah Girls handshake, which just tickles me to death, Galleria hugs us. "Smooches for the pooches!" she says. Every day she has a new saying, and we never know *what* to expect.

Galleria and Chanel are wearing such cute leotards! Angie and I look so plain, in our white shirts and black jeans. It'll be so nice when we can all dress alike all the time, like a real girl group. Yeah, right . . . like that'll ever happen.

"How's Porgy and Bess?" Chanel asks. She thinks it's cute that we have guinea pigs, because she isn't allowed to have any pets. She *loves* animals, too.

"They iz fine," Angie says, playing back.

"What do you feed them?" Dorinda asks.

"They love lettuce," I answer.

"Yeah, I bet—sprinkled with hot sauce!" Galleria blurts out, then looks at the door, because our dance teacher has arrived.

"Hi, I'm Raven Richards," says the teacher, who is real tall and skinny. She is wearing a red leotard and skirt, with a big black belt in the middle. None of us are tall like that. It must be real nice, having those long legs!

"Okay, let's get some combinations down," Raven says, moving her hips. "The movement in the hips is to a one-two, one-two-three combo. Okay, girls?"

Raven looks at me and adds, "Slink, don't bounce."

Raven? She looks more like Wes Craven! I say to myself, because she makes me so mad, embarrassing me like that in front of everybody. It's bad enough that Galleria is always on us about dancing, and Daddy is always on us about practicing more . . .

Dag on, I suddenly realize—she's right. I *am* bouncing!

After class, I feel real tired and sick. "Forget about buffalo wings—I could eat a whole buffalo right about now," I moan.

"That's funny. I thought you were on a seafood diet, Aqua," Galleria quips, pushing me with her backpack.

"Seafood?" I say, squinching up my nose. I just wanna go home and get into bed. I don't care if Kahlua never calls.

"Yeah, you *see* food, and you *eat* it!"

Galleria always makes me laugh. She is *real* funny.

"Don't be down, Aqua and Angie," she says then, holding my arm. "'Operation Kahlua' is in full effect. We just keep doing our thing, so that we're ready for Freddy. You know what I'm sayin'?"

"Yes, Galleria. We know what you're saying!" I answer, feeling a little better—at least good enough to get on the subway again and go home.

Chapter 9

Daddy is grinning from ear to ear when we get home. His job interview this morning must have gone well. See, he wants to leave his job as senior vice president of marketing at Avon. He and Ma decided that, since he used to be her boss, it wasn't a good idea that they work at the same company anymore.

"Daddy, how did the job interview go?" I ask. Angie and I sit down at the kitchen counter, and wait for Daddy to give us our dinner.

"I took the job," he says smiling. "Now I'm a SWAT man."

"That's real good, Daddy," I exclaim, then kiss him on the cheek. SWAT is the biggest bug repellent company in the country, he told us. They make all kinds of sprays for crawling insects, flying insects, lazy insects—you name it, they got a spray for it.

"Here's the campaign I'm gonna be working on," he says, pushing a black folder toward us. On the folder it has the company's slogan, *Flee, Flea, you hear me?*

Now Daddy is grinning and looking at us. I guess he wants us to say something funny about the slogan or something.

"What?" I ask, looking at him.

"That's not the best news I had all day," he says, still smiling like a Cheshire Cat who ate an insect.

"No?" Angie asks sheepishly.

"No. The best news I got just arrived in a phone call," he says, still smiling.

Daddy sure knows how to drag things out. When we were little, it used to take us two hours just to open our Christmas presents, because he would have to hand them to us first, then wait till *he* said to open them!

"Well, girls, maybe you should call your friend Galleria and find out for yourselves. She just called."

"Daddy, how could you wait so long to tell us?" I whine playfully. He always gets us real good with his tricks.

Angie and I jump up and down and hug each other, then I dial the phone, and she listens at the receiver.

When Galleria picks up the phone, she is yelling so loud, I can hardly understand her.

"Stop screaming, Galleria!"

Trying to catch her breath, Galleria says between gasps, "They're gonna give us a showcase in Los Angeles!!!"

"Hush your mouth!" I exclaim—the same thing Big Momma always says when she gets excited. "For real?"

"Wheel-a-deal for *real*!" Galleria retorts. "Kahlua and her moms told the Def Duck Records peeps that we were 'off the hook, snook,' and they said, 'Well, come on with it!'"

I'm not exactly sure what Galleria means, so I have to ask again, "Does that mean we got a record deal?"

"No, Aqua—just try and go with my flow. It *means* they'll fly us to Los Angeles, and arrange a showcase for us. They'll make sure all the right peeps are in the house to get a read on our

Cheetah Girl groove. There are no guarantees, but at least we get a free trip to Hey, ho, Hollywood!"

"Omigod, I think I'm gonna faint!" I scream into the phone receiver. Angie grabs it from me, to talk to Galleria herself. I stand in the middle of the kitchen with my hand on my forehead. Then I just hug Daddy, and start crying tears of gratitude. I can't believe I ever doubted what God had in store for us! Now, the rest is up to us.

"How'd you find out?" Angie asks Galleria, then yells to me and Daddy, "They called Ms. Dorothea at her store, and asked her if *we* would be *interested*. Can you believe that?"

"*Please*, I'll pack my bags and fly the plane right now myself!" I yell, so Galleria can hear me-and trying to sound like I'm not scared of airplanes, which I *am*.

Daddy gives me a look, like "We'll see how you feel when you get up in the air." That's all right—I'll take a whole box of Cloud Nine pills if I have to, to keep from getting sick on the plane. Hallelujah, thank you, Jesus, we are going to Hollywood!

Chapter 10

After we finish talking with Galleria, we go over the whole story again with Ms. Dorothea. Then, of course, we call Chanel, and after that, Dorinda. But we're only just crankin' up. We call Big Momma to share the news. And finally, we reach our Ma, who is in Seattle on business.

She is surprised to hear from us, because unless it's an emergency, we usually only talk on Sunday after church.

"But this *is* an emergency, Ma," I tell her, "because if I wake up tomorrow and find out this is all a dream, I'm gonna need mouth-to-mouth resuscitation!"

"Hush your mouth, Aqua," Ma says.

"You're gonna let us go, right?" I ask Ma nervously. She gets mad if we do things without asking her permission, even if we are living with Daddy. She says she's "still the boss of this house," no matter what Daddy thinks.

"You just make sure you do your homework while you're there, so you don't fall behind in school," Ma warns us. "But you go and have a good time. It's a shame the two of you haven't really been anywhere before this."

I feel like the whole world is right outside our front door, waiting for us. "That's all right, Ma—if things work out, we're going to be going *everywhere*—and we'll send plane tickets for you to come see us perform!"

"Well, for now, I think you'd better just get off the phone and go to bed, it's past your bedtime," Ma says sternly.

"Yes, ma'am, we're going right now. You wanna speak to Daddy?" I ask, hoping our good news will help them not be mad at each other—for at least a little while. As it is, I have to bite my tongue half the time, not to blurt and tell Ma about High Priestess Abala Shaballa.

"No, Aquanette, I don't have the time. I have

to finish some reports before I go to bed. I'm real proud of you, though. *Real* proud."

I don't even look at Daddy when I get off the phone, because I feel so bad Ma didn't want to talk to him.

"Good night, Daddy," I say, kissing him on the cheek.

"Good night, Daddy," Angie says, then kisses him on the other cheek. When I pass that scary-looking Bogo Mogo Warrior Mask on the way upstairs, I stick my tongue out at it, then poke Angie in the stomach, and we both start giggling.

"That's enough, y'all," Daddy says, leaning over his record collection in the living room. Daddy doesn't like us playing around before we go to bed—he wouldn't care if God came to the door and said it was okay. He likes peace and quiet when he's getting ready to play his music.

Angie and I spend another hour yakking in whispers about this most incredible day. When we're finally lying in bed, trying to get some sleep, I suddenly hear a noise in the bedroom closet!

"Angie, you hear that?" I whisper, sitting upright in my bed. "Lawd, you think that thing got out of the shoe boxes or something?"

We hear more scratching noises in the closet, and we both sit real quiet. "I don't care if it did, 'cuz I ain't going in there to find out!" Angie says, then hides under her covers.

It figures. That scaredy cat. Well, I ain't getting out of the bed either. They'll have to *drag* me out the bed before I get up and go look in that closet.

All of a sudden, I have the strangest thought. "Angie! You don't think that Teddy Bear Poodle thing brought us good luck, do you?"

"Maybe," Angie says, real quiet. "But I don't care—I'm just going to Hollywooooood!" she says, imitating Galleria.

"Not without me, you ain't!" I retort, and hide farther under the covers, till my feet are hanging out the bed. Feeling the cool air on my toes, I get a creepy feeling, and scrunch them back under the covers real quick. I'm not taking any chances—I mean, what if that thing in the closet is *hungry*?

Please God—make it stop raining! If it keeps

raining this hard much longer, Mighty Mouth Airlines will cancel our flight for sure!

Daddy keeps coming up to our room, to give us the latest weather report—like he's Sonny Shinbone, the weatherman on television. Daddy used to travel all over the country with his job at Avon, so I guess he *could* be a weatherman, but right now, he is "getting on our last good nerve," as Big Momma would say. I wish he would just stay downstairs with the 'sacred one,' so we can pack our suitcases in peace.

"'Furious Flo' is heading north," he says, hovering over us in our bedroom. 'Furious Flo' is this terrible tropical storm that started a few days ago in Florida, and is wreaking havoc all over the place.

She must be mighty mad, because she's making people lose their homes and everything, with all the water she's sending their way. Thank God, Big Momma called and says everything is okay in Houston. Daddy is pacing back and forth, wearing out our rug. He's making us more nervous than we already are!

"What if you don't have enough material to

perform?" Daddy asks, smoking his pipe. He must be *real* nervous, too, because he usually only smokes his pipe late at night, when he's listening to his music or watching television. I hope he doesn't drop any ashes on our white carpet. He's always fussing at *us* to be careful about staining the carpet, because it costs a lot of money to get it cleaned professionally.

"Daddy, we're not the only singers performing in the New Talent Showcase," I explain to him. "The record company does this all the time. They have scouts all over the country looking for new artists. Then they fly them to Los Angeles, and put them in a showcase in front of industry people. There'll probably be a lot of other singers there. We'll be lucky if we get to perform three songs."

"That's right," Angie adds. "They told us to have three songs to perform."

"Okay, okay, I'm just trying to understand how all this works," Daddy says, puffing on his pipe quietly—which means he's thinking about *something*. "You think maybe that magic spell Abala prepared for you girls had something to do with this stroke of luck?"

"Daddy!" I yell. "This is no stroke of luck! If

it wasn't for Galleria and Ms. Dorothea, we'd be packing to go to Big Momma's, and playing 'Tiptoe Through the Tulips' in her garden—*again*!"

Daddy gives me that stern look, like, "Don't get too grown for your britches."

"I'm just asking a question," he says. "Maybe the spell worked just a little late, that's all I'm saying."

Angie and I get real quiet.

"What's the name of the place where you're performing?" Daddy asks for the *hundredth* time!

"The Tinkerbell Lounge," I say quietly. "It's in West Hollywood, and we wrote down all the information on the paper on the kitchen table—*and* we gave it to Ma, too."

I carefully fold the leopard miniskirt and vest that Ms. Dorothea made for us, and put it in the suitcase. I'm just waiting for Daddy to say something else.

"You know, maybe you should bring the navy blue dresses you wore to church last Sunday."

I don't want to fight with him anymore. "Yes, Daddy," I mumble, then go to the closet to get the dresses he wants us to wear.

Thank God, Daddy walks out of our bedroom then, to go downstairs. Angie and I stop packing, and just plop down on our beds.

I'm so nervous, I'm sweating like a tree trunk. Angie and I look at each other, and I know we're thinking the same thing. Giggling, she jumps up and takes the navy blue dresses and sticks them back in the closet!

"No, silly willy," I exclaim, imitating Galleria, "stick those things in the *back* of the closet, so he doesn't see them if he comes snooping around our room while we're gone!"

"Yeah, that's if we get to go," Angie sighs, going over to the window to look at the rain.

"Well, let's pack our bathing suits just in case. Maybe they'll have a swimming pool or something."

Angie runs to the closet and gets out our bathing suits.

"Did you see anything strange in the back of the closet?" I ask her, kinda joking. But inside, I'm kinda serious. What if Daddy is right about Abala's magic spell? What if Mr. Teddy Poodly is running around in there?

That's when I remember something *real*

strange. "Remember, Angie, I took the Scotch tape off that shoe box?"

"Yeah," she says, smiling at me. "Maybe that's what High Priestess Abala Shaballa meant, when she said the Vampire Spell didn't work 'cuz we must not have followed her instructions."

"I don't get it," Angie says, shrugging her shoulders.

"I put Scotch tape on the shoe box in the first place. She didn't tell us to do that. Maybe that's why the spell didn't work! Maybe Mr. Teddy Poodly could only do his thing when he was able to get out of the box!"

"Well, there has to be *some* reason why those boys won, because they sure weren't *that* good. Not as good as we are," Angie says, sitting on the bed and crossing her legs Indian style.

"Yeah. I know that's right. When did I take the Scotch tape off my shoe box?"

"I don't know. After we came home from the Apollo, I guess," Angie says.

"That's right. It *does* seem kinda strange that this happened—"

"Well, nothing *has* happened, Aquanette. I mean, we don't know what's gonna happen when we get out there. They didn't say they're gonna give us a record deal or anything."

I can tell Angie is getting exasperated. And I know what's wrong, too. She is being stubborn because she wants to stay mad at High Priestess Abala Shaballa.

Neither one of us is happy about Daddy getting a girlfriend so quick. Dag on, he and Ma just broke up! Okay, it's been a year, but that's *nothing*. And why did he have to pick *her*?

"I'm just saying, Angie, that maybe we're wrong about Abala," I say, giving my sister that look.

Angie just drags the suitcase off the bed. "We going, or what?"

"Let's ask Daddy and find out," I say, trailing behind her down the stairs. "Daddy! Can you help us with the luggage, please?"

High Priestess Abala Shaballa comes to the bottom of the stairwell. "Your father is on the phone with the airline, checking to make sure your flight isn't canceled," she says, looking like she feels bad for us if we don't get to go.

When we put the luggage by the front door, she turns and winks at us, "I see the Vampire

Spell worked, no?" Her eyes get real squinty, like a mouse's! I never noticed that before.

"Let's go, before the airline changes their mind," Daddy says chuckling, then hustles us out the door and into the Bronco.

The traffic is so bad going to the airport, I don't think we're ever going to get there! I'm really sweating now. "Angie, are you hot?"

"Yeah," Angie says, then sighs. "It's the traffic in New York. It makes me *nervous*, too. I didn't even know they made so many cars!"

"I don't know. It gets pretty crowded in Houston around rush hour," Daddy says, not looking up from the wheel.

Finally, we arrive at the airport, and by now, I'm dying of thirst.

"Did you pack some water, Angie?"

"Yes, Ma!" she says all huffy.

"Daddy, don't forget to feed Porgy and Bess," I mumble. All of a sudden, I'm feeling real jumpy. "They're real particular about their food—they only like fresh lettuce, and they don't like their water too cold."

"Yes, Aquanette, I'll take them for walks too," Daddy says, rolling one of our suitcases through the airport terminal.

"There's Ms. Dorothea!" I say, waving my arm so she can see us. She has on a cheetah coat and big cheetah hat, and is standing with Mr. Garibaldi.

Then she moves aside a little, and I see that they're not alone. "Oh, there's Galleria, too!" Galleria looks so small next to her mother. She is wearing a cheetah coat and hat, too.

"Don't they look like a cheetah and a cub together?" I joke to Angie.

"They sure do!"

"My, she is tall," High Priestess Abala Shaballa comments about Ms. Dorothea.

I wanna say to her High-Mightyness, "Yeah, well, at least she don't put hexes on people like you do!" But I keep my mouth shut, because I'm not so mad at her anymore.

People are looking at us, probably because of all the fabric Abala has wrapped on her body and head. They probably think she's African royalty or something like that.

"There's Chanel and Dorinda," Angie says, pointing to where they're standing by the window. When Chanel and Dorinda see us, they come running over with Galleria and Ms. Dorothea.

"*Pooches gracias* for showing up!" Chanel giggles, then we all hug each other, screaming and carrying on.

Everybody is looking at us now. Daddy gives us a look, like, "calm down."

"Let me check at the reservation desk and make sure the flight is on time," he says, holding the High Priestess's arm.

"You didn't pack any crawfish in there, did you?" Galleria asks, teasing us.

"No, because Porgy and Bess ate 'em!" I chuckle back.

"I miss Toto already," Galleria whines.

"How come you didn't bring him?" I ask.

"We're going to Los Angeles for a singers' showcase, not a Poodle Convention, darling," Ms. Dorothea quips, but I can tell she feels guilty about leaving him behind. Galleria told us her mother gets hysterical if Toto chokes on a dog biscuit or anything.

"Dad is gonna take care of him," Galleria says, then turns to Mr. Garibaldi, "right, Dad?'

"*Sì, cara, sì!* " Mr. Garibaldi chuckles. He has on one of those real funny hats that looks like a raccoon, or something furry like that.

I look away, to see that Daddy is walking toward us wearing the longest face.

"Oh, no," I moan.

"The flight is canceled," Daddy announces.

I just want to fall on the floor and pull a temper tantrum. Dag on, we can't take any more disappointments!

"But they've put the six of you on stand-by, in case they can get you on a later flight," Daddy says, delivering the bad news like Granddaddy Walker does when he's telling a family he can't make a corpse at the funeral parlor look real good.

"Whatever makes them clever," Galleria says, disappointed. "I guess their mouth ain't mighty enough for Furious Flo."

"Well, we ain't going home," I announce adamantly. "I don't care if we have to stay in the airport all night."

"I know that's right," Angie pipes in.

"Don't worry, darlings," Ms. Dorothea says, putting her arms around us. "It's just another wrong turn on the road, and we've landed in hyena territory once again—but when the hyenas have eaten their fill, they'll leave us alone, and then we'll be on our merry way.

All's we gotta do is click our heels and *pray.*"

Chanel starts clicking her heels together. They are real cute vinyl sandals, and have goldfish in the heels that you can see—but they do make her feet look kinda wet.

"I don't know how you could wear those goldfish on your feet in this weather, Chuchie," Galleria says, rolling her eyes. "Oh, I get it, maybe you'll be able to swim upstream if the water gets too high!"

Chanel is too crestfallen to care what Galleria says. "I hope we have somewhere to swim to," she mumbles.

We all drag our luggage to the check-in storage room. Galleria and Ms. Dorothea's cheetah luggage is so pretty. Ours looks kinda ugly next to theirs. It's just plain ol' blue vinyl. When Angie and I get some money, we're gonna buy ourselves pretty luggage too. I wonder if we are ever gonna get some money of our own. Not soon enough, that's for sure!

After we eat some hamburgers and french fries at Pig in the Poke Restaurant, we get real sleepy, and head to the waiting area, where we sit on the ugly vinyl chairs. "How come they don't have real velvet chairs or something?" Chanel moans.

I put my coat on the floor so I can lie down. "Sweet dreams," Chanel coos. She seems so sad.

I can't take the noise anymore. People are walking around like they're in a hurry, but I know they're going nowhere. All this is making me *real* sleepy.

I don't know how long we've been sleeping, but I hear a loud noise, and I think it's in my dreams, but then I realize it's an announcer's voice on the loudspeaker. "Mrs. Gari-bolda, please come to the reservation desk. Mrs. Gari-bolda, please come to the reservation desk."

"Mom, wake up!" Galleria says, shaking her mother. Ms. Dorothea jumps up, like one of the creatures from *Night of the Living Dead.*

"Wait here!" she orders.

"What time is it?" Chanel says, rubbing her eyes open.

"It's ten o'clock. We've been waiting for four hours," Galleria answers. Then, humming aloud, she sings, "Rain or shine, all is mine. . . ."

We look at each other real quiet. It feels like we're waiting to see if we won the $64,000 prize on the game show *My Dime, Your Time!*

Running toward us, Ms. Dorothea announces, "Come on, Cheetah Girls! It's time to head for Hollywood!"

We all jump out of our chairs and let out a cheer. Then we gather our stuff, and say good-bye to Daddy and Abala. The High Priestess kisses me on the forehead, and says, "Look for the Raven when she opens her wings."

"I will, Abala," I say. Yeah, right. Whatever.

Galleria is trying not to smirk, and as we're running through the terminal to keep up with Ms. Dorothea, she spreads her arms out and coos, "Caw! Caw! I'm the raven! Nevermore! Nevermore!"

Everybody is looking at us as we give our tickets to the attendant, giggling up a storm.

"Oh, and by the way, darling, tell that dreary announcer of yours it's Mrs. *Garibaldi*!" Ms. Dorothea tells the attendant.

"Ooh, this is dope!" Dorinda says, looking at the red velvet seats we pass in the first class section. She has never been on a plane before.

"This is where all the rich people sit," I whisper in Dorinda's ear. The flight attendants are giving out newspapers and bubbly-looking drinks in plastic cups to the first-class passengers.

"Momsy poo, can we sit in first class?" Galleria asks, giggling.

"Do you have first class money? You can sit there, darling poo, when *you're* paying."

We go back farther, and get to a section where there are more seats—and they're a *lot* smaller.

"Hold your breath, girls, and tuck it in," Galleria giggles as she sits down.

"Do' Re Mi, *mamacita,* you take the window seat," Chanel says to Dorinda. Bless her heart, she won't be able to see much out the window, even though the rain has stopped. It's so dark out now. But it was still nice of Chuchie to give her the seat. After we settle in, a pilot's voice comes over the loudspeaker and welcomes us aboard.

"*Hola, hola,* everybody, the Cheetah Girls are in the house!" Chanel coos. The lady in the row across from me and Angie looks at us in curiosity. How'd she get her hair teased so high in this weather? I wonder.

"She looks like she's ready for takeoff!" Galleria whispers to me. She is seated in the row behind me.

A screen gets pulled down by the flight attendant, and a movie explains all about safety, and what to do if something happens.

I start getting *real* scared, and my hands are sweating. But I have plenty of time to calm down. We sit and wait in the plane for *two hours*!

Finally, the captain announces that we are "ready for takeoff." Everyone in the plane starts clapping.

"We're ready for Freddy, yo!" Dorinda says, and lets out a hoot. She is so excited. For someone who's never been on a plane before, she seems so much calmer than we do.

I reach down to get my Cloud Nine pills out of my carry-on bag, and put them in the flap in front of my seat. Just in case I get sick, I don't want to be barfing up a storm and embarrassing myself in front of my friends.

Galleria starts singing: "Snakes in the grass have no class/But cheetah girls have all the swirls."

We join in, singing together, and people start clapping all around us, cheering us on.

When the plane finally starts ascending into the air, though, we get real quiet. I think we're all pretty scared.

When we finally reach cruising altitude, I let out a sigh of relief. "We're going to Hollywood!" I yell.

"Hey, we never did get to see the Sandman at the Apollo, did we?" Galleria turns and asks me, then chuckles. "I was kinda disappointed."

"Don't be, Miss Galleria," I say, laying on my Southern accent and fluttering my eyelashes, "If we turn 'stinkeroon like loony toons' at the Tinkerbell Lounge, neither Freddy nor the Sandman is gonna be able to help us—'cuz *Captain Hook* is gonna yank us off the stage himself!!!"

But I just know that ain't gonna happen. We all know it. Maybe it's High Priestess Abala Shaballa's spell, or maybe it's God's Way, just that we know we're due—whatever. It really doesn't matter. What matters is that we're the Cheetah Girls, and we've got growl power. It's only a matter of time till the whole world knows it.

So hey, ho, Hollywooood, the Cheetah Girls are looking gooood!

More Pounce to the Ounce

We wuz walking down the street
eating Nestlé's Crunch
when a big baboon
tried to get a munch.
Please don't ask for bite
'cuz that's my lunch
Times are hard and
you should know the deal
So please stop breathing
on my "Happy Meal."
Here's the wrapper
take the crumbs
Next time you try to sneak a chomp
you won't get none!!!
Snakes in the grass have no class
but cheetah girls have all the swirls.
Big baboons don't make us swoon
'cuz Cheetah Girls can reach the moon

To all the competition, what can we say?
You'd better bounce, y'all

'cuz every Cheetah has its day
You'd betta bounce, y'all
While you still got some flounce, y'all
'cuz Cheetah Girls are gonna pounce, y'all
and we got more pounce to the ounce *y'all*

More Pounce to the Ounce
We don't eat lunch
More Pounce to the Ounce
Come on with the brunch!

The Cheetah Girls Glossary

Angling for an intro: When you're cheesing for the purpose of an introduction to someone.

At the bottom of the crab barrel: When you're down in the dumps.

Churl: A word made up by combining "girl" and "child" together.

Corpse: The body of a dead person. A cadaver.

Crispy: Supertasty "flow" or food.

Diva size: Size fourteen and up.

Flounce: Show off.

Groovy like a movie: Dope. Cool.

Heffa: A girl who thinks she's all that and a bag of "juju beans."

Hex: A witchcraft spell.

Hush your mouth!: An affectionate response that's really asking, "Is that right?"

Monologue: A dramatic sketch performed by

an actor—or a "drama queen" kind of person.

Off the hook: Dope. Cool

Outtie like Snouty: When a situation gets a little cuckoo and you need a time-out break.

Passed: When someone dies.

Pouncing: A very important Cheetah Girl skill for taking control of a situation and making things happen.

Ready for Freddy: Ready for anything. Ready to do your thing.

She takes the cobbler: When someone is really too much. Can also be used like, "He gave me a C in math. That really takes the cobbler!"

Stinkeroon like loony toons: When you're having an off day with your "flow."

Wefties: Weaves that are so tick tacky the tracks are showing!

Wreckin' my flow: When something is interfering with your ability to talk, sing, think, or whatever it is you're trying to do.

PHOTO BY CHARLIE PIZZARELLO

ABOUT THE AUTHOR

Deborah Gregory earned her growl power as a diva-about-town contributing writer for ESSENCE, VIBE, and MORE magazines. She has showed her spots on several talk shows including OPRAH, RICKI LAKE, and MAURY POVICH. She lives in New York City with her pooch, Cappuccino, who is featured as the Cheetah Girls' mascot, Toto.

PHOTO BY TREVOR BROWN

JUMP AT THE SUN